T0356280

Published by Semiotext(e)
PO Box 629, South Pasadena, CA 91031
www.semiotexte.com

Cover photograph: Raphael Chatelain
Design: Hedi El Kholti
ISBN: 978-1-63590-238-9

10 9 8 7 6 5 4 3 2 1

Printed and bound in the United States of America
Distributed by the MIT Press, Cambridge, MA.

NAME

Constance Debré

**Translated by
Lauren Elkin**

Semiotext(e)

1

She dips the washcloth in the bowl of warm water, she passes it over his face, she lowers the sheet, she lowers his pajama trousers, she passes the washcloth over my father's inert penis, she raises the sheet above his waist, she asks me for a shirt, I turn to the wardrobe, I lay one on the bed, she takes my father by the shoulders, she tries to remove his pajama top, his arms don't bend, she tries harder, I see she's trying harder, I lean forward, Go on, lean forward, I catch hold of his cold shoulder, I slip my arm behind his cold back, I put my hand in his cold hand, I pull on the arm that is stuck, I think of rigor mortis, I remove his pajama top, I put on the new shirt, I lay my father back against the pillow, she puts away the two pumps, she takes out the tubes, she cleans up the packets of morphine and sedatives, she puts them in a special briefcase with a code, she came to collect the morphine, that's why she's here, It's part of the procedure, she says, the washcloth the shirt was her idea, We can't leave him like that, she says, she leaves, it's still dark out, I go back to the kitchen, I make some more coffee, it's almost morning, the light is beautiful, I inhale the dry odor of the garden, at eight thirty I take my father's bank card from the chimney, I take the Peugeot, the 206 three-door hatchback diesel with 197,000 kilometers on it bought at Touraine Used Cars a few days ago, I go to the ATM at the Super U, I hesitate, How much, I take out €200.

It is already warm out when I get back, I close the shutters in the bedroom, I look at him, he already looks different, more drawn, more waxy, the undertakers will come when the doctor gives us the death certificate, they really shouldn't wait with this heat, I stay in the house as it gets hotter, I am alone with him, like last night, like all the nights these past few weeks, it's calm, it's new this calm, it's the quiet of the oxygen machine that's no longer going, sometimes I go to his room, I go in, I look at him.

The doctor knocks at the door, I let him in, he goes in the bedroom, he records the death, we go to the living room, he fills out the certificate, he says that he liked my father, that he was a bit challenging as a patient but he liked him a lot, I think he must say that every time, about every dead patient, that he must think people like that, he takes me in his arms, it's awkward, I'm stiff, it doesn't last, he gives me the certificate, Get out, get out do you hear me, he gets out.

My sister arrives with her husband, she's wearing sunglasses like at a celebrity funeral, she's crying, she doesn't dare go in to see him, I go with her, they have lunch, I don't, I want to go swimming, usually I go earlier, the undertakers arrive, they park their truck in front of the house, there's two or three of them I'm not sure, only men, maybe it's a man's job, I give them the certificate, I sign some papers, my sister goes back into my father's bedroom, I hear them talking to her, she's crying hard, she says through her tears that she doesn't want them to take him away, I go in or her husband does I don't remember, we talk to her, she calms down, I tell them to go, to go home, they live nearby, on the other side of the Loire, they left Paris, I tell them I'll look after the undertakers, you guys should get out of here, they go, the undertaker guys take the metal stretcher out of their truck, I wonder if it's refrigerated, they go to the bedroom, I give them some clothes for the coffin, I give them a pair of jeans, another blue shirt, a pair of Clarks, some underpants, some socks, I go outside, into the street in front of the house, they go through the door with my father in the opaque plastic body bag, it's transparent, I see my father's white hair, they slide my father into the back of the truck, they leave, him too, I go back into the house, I'm alone, the house is empty, it's sunny, I go into his bedroom, I look, I move into the living room, I take my pool bag, I go back out, I take the Peugeot, Touraine Used Cars is just down a bit, on the levee, in the industrial zone by the river, I drive, it's a beautiful day, I cross the Cher, I make the turn toward Tours Nord, I park in the lot of the Centre aquatique du Lac, a fifty-meter pool, I swim every day, I swim.

2

I was born to do the dirty work, I say dirty but I think beautiful, beautiful work, the most just, the most moral, I insist on that, the most moral, that of destroying, finishing. I say this calmly, simply, just that which has to be done, what we all have to do, not repairing, like they're always telling us, there is nothing to repair, but on the contrary breaking, leaving, taking part in the great business of loss, accelerating it, finishing things. What is your name? My name is Nobody, a name is nothing, like family, like childhood, I don't believe in it, I don't want it.

In the death room, in a drawer, a photograph of a baptism. An official photo of my official life. In front of my mother's chateau in Basque country, my parents, my two grand-mothers, my grandfather the prime minister, me in my mother's arms, wearing an oversized dress made of white lace. There was an article in the local newspaper, at Mass the men of the village sang for me, the president of the republic told my grandfather that Constance is a beautiful name. It's like in a choose-your-own-adventure story, you have to decide to go right or go left, decide which story to tell, which hero to play, sort, decide, get out. All photos are like that, all language as well I imagine. I don't take the photograph, I put it back in this desk which will be sold, or taken home by my sister, or thrown away, I close the drawer, I leave the room.

I have rid myself of nearly everything. Of family, marriage, work, apartments, belongings, people. That's what I've spent the last few years doing, ridding myself. All at once and very calmly, it's been both fast and slow, physical and internal, it's been like digging, like going down into the tunnels, from one underground space to another, like swimming, too, like doing lap after lap. You can't go backward, what existed before is gone, what you were before is gone, it's this impossibility you're after. To make all the questions go away, deprive them of reason, make them obsolete. You can refuse an inheritance, I'm not talking about money, it's been a long time now since I had any, I'm talking about faith, loyalty. Let's do away with origins, I don't hold on to the corpses.

3

The setting: 1960s Paris, Saint-Germain-des-Prés, full of sons and daughters from good families. On my mother's side there were four sisters, just as on my father's side four brothers, the same madness on each side of the family because families are always mad. She was the youngest, born in a château. When they met she was living in a large apartment on the rue Bonaparte, with the sister closest in age, the one who's going to die of alcohol and pills. Overdose or suicide, hard to tell in these cases. The building belonged to her family, to their family, to my family, in the entrance hall there was a marble bust of an ancestral baron and they had cousins on every floor. Her own father, my grandfather, died when she was fourteen, he was also an MP, a government minister even, but he had been dead for a long time. Her mother, my grandmother, lived in the southwest with her dogs, and came to Paris from time to time to check up on what was happening. There were arguments, screams, scenes. Everyone in that family was violent. Aristocracy makes you crazy. Not because of the inbreeding, but because of faith. Faith that it is real, being noble. Especially when it no longer is, especially when everybody dies and the châteaus are burning. In that family they raised children like they raised horses, to be beautiful. Being beautiful meant lots of different things. The rest was of no importance.

After the bac, after all those years at boarding school with the nuns, she signed up for classes at the Sorbonne, when she was stopped in the street. They offered to take her picture, she posed for magazines, walked in runway shows, became a model, there was something terrifying in her beauty, for everyone, for her as well.

When she comes to pick me up from school, ten or fifteen years later, that is what I see. Among the other mothers, normal and ridiculous, she is taller, thinner, with her big coats and sunglasses. Even the fat unruly spaniel at the end of his leash only makes her look more royal. She could have gone around walking a pig and everyone would find it perfectly normal, even sublime. Everyone makes way for her when she walks down the street, it's like they feel compelled to bow to her, or to carry the hem of her coat, or to adopt the most sophisticated protocol, like in the empire of China in the first few pages of *René Leys*. I am amazed they even manage to address her directly, they even sometimes call her *tu*. She calls everyone *tu*. She is very warm. Never a snob. Keep it simple, she says to anyone who never manages it. Proust's Duchesse de Parme. They all fall under her spell. Everyone. I see it. It grabs hold of them. It's physical. They are no longer quite themselves. My friends, my friends' parents, the baker, a bum, it doesn't matter who, she turns them all to jelly.

When I am with her, I watch things happen, it never fails. The way they desire her. A crazy, respectful desire. You don't fuck a queen up against a wall. You may think of nothing else, but you don't touch her. You hope that she will lower herself to your level. That she will lower herself and fuck you. My mother always enjoys it. She parades her sovereign desire throughout the world. To be her child is to be sexual before anything else, because she is. To get hard and to come, to be frustrated and perverse, voyeur and pimp, calm and furious. I am a witness or an accomplice, I watch people fall beneath her gaze, I am the favorite son or daughter, I am the crown prince, *tu quoque mi fili*, "you too, my child?" I delight in it I am enraged by it, I am biding my time.

Now, when I look back, I think she was crazy. I've thought so for a few years now. Since I started dating women. Since I came to understand that all women are stark raving mad.

4

Staying in a studio, staying at a friend's place, staying at a lover's place, not having a home, not having a domicile, changing, moving, keeping nothing domestic, not being domestic, not sitting down, eating standing up, working in bed, changing places, changing beds, not having a bed, not having a cupboard, not having a bookshelf, throwing out books, not having much clothing, exercising, swimming, running, shaving your head, tattooing your body, seducing, being seduced, leaving, being left, training, improving, starting over, risking, wanting, doing, not crying, being beautiful, being a hero, that's how I'm living now.

Recently I've been staying near Montparnasse. It used to be a hotel. A table a mattress a pot. A coffee maker a knife a fork a cup. Some clothing, black or grey or white, my uniform, you could say, because I'm a soldier.

Everything I own fits in two bags, when they start to overflow I throw something away, that's the rule, the moral rule, the aesthetic rule. My room is between Daguerre and Froidevaux. I'm there but I'm not, I'm often elsewhere, on my bike, in the Métro, in the street, in the cafés, in the pools, in other people's apartments, which people lend me when they go away, or across the street, at the Savoy, forty euros a night, single bed, communal shower, when a girl stays over I would rather leave her my room because I don't sleep. I can be anywhere, it doesn't matter at all.

Walk into the void, that's it, that's what you have to do, get rid of everything, of everything you have, of everything you know, and go toward the unknown. Otherwise you're not alive, you think you are but you're not, you stay home with your knickknacks and spend your life not living. It's nothing less that that, what you have to do. What matters isn't being on the left or on the right, rich or poor, straight or gay, living in a studio or a château, owning or renting, being married or not, none of it matters at all, like it doesn't matter if you're a woman, or Black or white, from a family of government ministers or addicts or an orphan, if you're guilty or innocent, all of that means nothing, being free has nothing to do with all that clutter, with having suffered or not, being free is the void, it is only your relationship to the void.

Today I have a body. It took years. It's not an idea, it's not rhetoric, it's a fact that can be verified by looking in the mirror. My body appeared when I became a writer, when I became a lesbian, when I let go of some things and then lost the rest. Specifically in my muscles and my tendons, in my face and the bones in my skull. It's not my name that interests me but my body. You have to be very focused, very serious, when you live like that.

5

Still in Paris, still on the Left Bank, a little farther south, between Montparnasse and Saint-Michel. It's the late '70s. I'm playing in the Jardin du Luxembourg or the Jardins de l'Observatoire right nearby. I go to public school on the rue Saint-Jacques. There are Portuguese kids in my class, Spanish kids, French kids, an Arab kid who's the son of the mechanic on the boulevard Saint-Michel, a Black girl called Fatou, a Vietnamese girl who was adopted and who has a French first name, her mother teaches history and geography, I think, otherwise it's full of average white French kids from the neighborhood, the children of shopkeepers mostly, one or two doctors' kids, GPs no doubt. The streets are called Gay-Lussac, Herschel, l'Abbé-de-l'Épée. At this time the fifth is a neighborhood for professors, shopkeepers, and students, neither rich nor poor, normal Paris for the time, middle class, with its ugly cafés, Turkish toilets, the smell of cold tobacco, lemon-meringue tarts in the bakery windows, its gas stations, its cars that stink of gas, the buildings are mostly blackened, Paris is still dirty. Children from families like my own don't go to the public schools in the fifth, they go to private schools, to Stan, the Francs-Bourgeois, the Cours Désir, sometimes they wear uniforms, navy-blue smock dresses and long flannel shorts, English shoes with straps for girls and laces for the boys. The 1970s is between two eras, there are bourgeois people who still dress like it, my uncles never wear jeans, my cousins are not allowed to wear sneakers except in athletic situations. My parents are nothing like their brothers sisters cousins families, they live differently, they dress differently, they read different books, they think different thoughts. I'm not like my cousins either, or like other girls really. I dress like the boys, the ones from my neighborhood, from my school, more or less. My best friend is called Benjamin. His mother and grandmother run a home-decorations store on the boulevard Saint-Michel called Home Confort, next to a motorcycle store. He's like my brother, we're always together, in class, after school, during the holidays. He comes to Touraine with us, I go to Picardy with him, to Rouvroy-les-Merles where there's only one road, two farms, and the farmer's daughter who got pregnant when she was thirteen. He is calm like me. Calmer I think. I am calm to the point of rage, sometimes. We play marbles, LEGO, G.I. Joe, we make models, when we're a little older we go roller-skating, we go to cafés, play pinball, other arcade games. I have a BB gun, a Pneuma-Tir, so do my two cousins on my mother's side whom I see on the weekends. On Saturdays we're alone, we can do what we like, their mother who is my mother's cousin works in a shop since she got divorced. They are a kind of gang, we roam the neighborhood in roller stakes with our Pneuma-Tirs, I am the only girl in the group of boys, everyone is used to it.

My parents think it's important for me to go to public school. My mother says we have to be modern, live like everyone else. She says that it was a shock for her to leave boarding school after the bac, to discover the world. As if she had been raised in a cult, like in those stories about Mormon kids. For my father, public school is a given.

They smoke opium at night. They lie down. There is an oil lamp that casts an orange light, Chinese pillows made of lacquered wood on which to rest your head, long pipes, needles with which they prepare the little ball above the lamp, before placing it in the pipe to be smoked. They each do this for the other. I see them sometimes, when I get up, when I can't sleep. I can't sleep because I have asthma or I have asthma because I can't sleep. The pipes are beautiful. They are in the living room, on a piece of black ebony furniture, an Italian writing desk, or was it Portuguese, with hunting scenes inlaid in ivory. During the day I put my nose to the bowl of a terra cotta pipe, it's cold and smooth, the color of brick, a little darkened by the flame. Heroin doesn't smell like anything—medicine, Néo-Codion, Stilnox, Tranxene, Valium, none of them smell like anything. Alcohol stinks and makes bodies stink. But opium is good, even just to smell it.

6

We're in the car, we park, she cuts the engine, she turns around and from the back seat she pulls out some strawberries and cream, or was it a pastry, she says that my aunt loves sweet things, she says she won't be long, I wait for my mother in the car, I watch the people, I think, Sainte-Anne is a good place for thinking, like the Santé on the other side of the wall, the crazy people on one side, the guilty on the other. I will spend time at the Santé much later when I am a lawyer, to see the people I'm defending, to prepare their interrogations, their hearings, their requests to be freed which always fail because justice is pointless, I will return to Sainte-Anne to see my father when he comes for detox, which will always fail because that's pointless too. My mother returns, she tells me my aunt is hearing voices, General de Gaulle, Napoleon, Joan of Arc, all the classics. My aunt has always been crazy about politics, we have to save France or the Basque

Country or take revenge on the people who handed her father over to the Germans. Often she talks about her book, she will talk about it for years, she's always in the middle of writing it and it will explain everything.

My crazy aunt has six children. She left them in the Virgin Islands. The British Virgin Islands. Antigua Saint Kitts. Not Guadeloupe Martinique. They speak English, they always speak English in that family. One of them has Down syndrome and is going to die. My uncle is Black. He's a lawyer and speaks Oxford English, but still Black. I can imagine what a scene that must have caused, in their racist family. Now that she's crazy, and everything else has fallen apart, nobody cares, it's no longer the real problem. She's crazy, but hardly more so than the others if you think about it, with their illusions about nobility, family, France, with their alcoholism, which they pretend not to notice. Apart from the voices, of course. Apart from the fact that she sometimes gets herself arrested, obviously. And that she'll end up in Sainte-Anne or elsewhere.

The second sister is mean. Hysterical like the others. She also had a daughter who died. We don't keep count of the dead in my mother's family. We barely notice the insanity, we no longer bother looking for the cause.

The third one is more of an alcoholic than the others, to the point of drinking eau de cologne in the château bathrooms. She got pregnant when she was sixteen. They worked something out with the boy's family. A good family. They hid the pregnancy. After the baby was born it was sent to a babysitter in Spain, they came to get it later, after a year or two. My cousin was raised all over the place. My aunt couldn't keep it together. She drank too much. They say that my cousin was difficult. It's difficult to be a bastard in this family. Then my aunt died. Maybe that's what helped my cousin survive.

There were four of them, my mother and her sisters. Today, they're all dead. My mother was the youngest. The elder sisters were born in Paris before the war, the younger ones in Basque Country, in U. They grew up in the château. Then in Paris, avenue Paul-Doumer, in a big apartment. There were always loads of servants. They spent all their vacations in Basque Country. My mother had an Irish nanny whom they called Miss and whose name I never knew. When she was eight they sent her to boarding school like her sisters. That's what they did with children. You thrust them into the nanny's arms and then you stuck them in boarding school. I don't know where they ever would have experienced tenderness. Maybe with the nannies. It's also sad when the nannies die. But we don't cry for the servants. We store up our sadnesses, we don't cry, we go crazy.

My cousin A. died when she was two, she drowned in an inflatable pool. My uncle went to answer the phone, he was only away a minute or two. My aunt and uncle split up not long after.

My cousin S., my crazy aunt's daughter, the one with Down syndrome, died when she was in her twenties. I don't know if people with Down syndrome always die young. I don't know if we still say *people with Down syndrome*.

My uncle E., my mother's cousin, age eighteen, car accident coming home from a family party at a family château.

My aunt M., my mother's cousin, age forty, cancer.

My nephew LJ, twenty-two, overdose.

There are others.

In my mother's family there's a small collection of dead people who died young or violently.

I would like it to be beyond the shadow of a doubt, for it to be completely clear, that when I say I rejoice in the dead, I rejoice at the dead. Respect for the dead is the most disgusting thing there is, even respect in general, there is nothing to respect.

7

Jeans, black loafers or Clarks, blue Oxford shirts; a tie, always; a blazer; a jacket; sometimes a turtleneck; sometimes a leather jacket, never a coat; his cigarettes; his slimness; his pallor; his gray eyes, my father is always elegant. He doesn't have many clothes, he buys them at the first shop he sees. Elegant without thinking about it, elegant because he doesn't care. Even now, even old, even in his pajamas like last summer at the hospital for his tongue cancer, even in the country in his putrid house in a dirty sweater and his supermarket jeans, with his oxygen tank, his pacemaker, his Subutex and his morphine, even with his poverty, filth, aging, and death, my father is elegant. Elegant in not giving a fuck about anything, clothes, money, himself, and everyone else. Never asking any questions, never saying anything. Elegant in never being there. For the past few months if anyone bothered him about anything he'd say Leave me the fuck alone I'm dying here.

Before he said nothing, he just took a hit or some whiskey without looking anywhere in particular. His decline has lasted thirty years. Or maybe forty, or fifty, it's hard to say. For a long time, it was the fire brigade, melodrama, one crisis after another. For the past decade or so hardly anything has happened, it's all been so slow, like tai chi. He hardly moves from his armchair, looks straight at the TV. To his left, the fireplace, with its mountain of ash, full of burned-out old yogurt pots, ice cream wrappers, medicine, everything he tosses in there. The house is overflowing with broken things and dust, the garden full of weeds and too-heavy branches that always succumb to their weight, as if his indoor space were spreading outside. It is his obsession with abandonment, impotence as will, that's why we can never intervene, it is impossible to repair anything, and so to spend time in this house is to spend time with the dust and the cold, the iced-over radiators, the chipped plates, the missing lightbulbs, the dead sockets, the busted-up tiles. The Montlouis aesthetic is an aesthetic of the garbage dump, with everything frozen somewhere between sinking and resisting, but it isn't clear if the two effects—annihilation and invincibility—will find a synthesis. From time to time, in Paris, those who know him will ask how he is. They are thinking of the charming guy they haven't seen in thirty years. *Charming*, they say. I don't say *charming*, if I said *charming* I too would remain at a distance from him. From the void. From the violence of the void. He doesn't say a word about it. There is nothing to be said. These kinds of things are solitary. Kindness surrounds us, it's peripheral, it supports us. Extreme kindness, even; politeness; tact. These things dwell on the surface of the life he does not inhabit, one he does not care about. I rarely see my father, I don't speak to him very often, I don't call him. In any case that's exactly what he asks for, that we leave one another alone. When you think about it, it's all right that way. He doesn't tell me anything and I don't tell him anything either. I treat him the way he treats everything, I shrug my shoulders and go on my way.

He is all that remains of my childhood, with his oxygen, his Subutex, and his illness in the falling-down house in Touraine. Luckily that house will not come to me. I will not inherit anything. The two armchairs, the photographs, I relinquish it all to my sister in advance. I don't speak to her anymore. In a few months perhaps, this whole story will be completely over. That's why I'm waiting for him to die. It is happening unbearably slowly.

When they met, he was finishing his law degree and starting a career in journalism. He lived in a studio on the rue Grégoire de Tours, above a greasy Greek joint called Zorba. His father, my grandfather, the one whose name I bear, had been prime minister. He wrote the Constitution. Headed up one ministry after another—defense, finance, justice, foreign affairs, that kind of thing. As a young man my father had his own bedroom in Matignon. He had three brothers, one older and two younger. He wasn't interested in his family, or in family stories, or in speeches about the family or France. He was nothing like the rest of them. Sometimes a person is born into a family they don't resemble at all. He spent his childhood with his nose in a book so he wouldn't have to see or hear them. He wanted to escape. He wanted to be Kessel, Monfreid, Albert Londres, not Paul Reynaud, not Charles Bovary. His earliest reporting was in Africa, then Asia. Wherever there were wars. Violence and beauty, it's always the same story. Drugs, too.

He's a journalist, he travels, he writes books. He talks. The Opium Wars. Speeches at the House of Commons. Chinese dynasties. The opium dens of Toulon. The Second Empire. Dylan. Rimbaud. Malaparte. Malcolm Lowry. *We'll to the Woods No More*. Norman Mailer. Painters too. A thousand other things. His gentle voice. He joins my games. I build my worlds with him. My LEGO, my forts, my costumes, our stories. We build worlds. My father understands childhood.

Africa and then Asia. Wars. Biafra, Vietnam, Cambodia, Mao's China. He knows each of these countries, their ancient cultures, their histories, he says that *we're* the barbarians. He can talk about it all for hours. He leaves as soon as he can. He is always leaving. My father watches everything with his gray eyes, he talks about the world, about books, but when it comes to himself, he keeps quiet, he takes off.

What does it do to you to see all of that, dead bodies, children with enormous bellies, bush hospitals, the smell of blood, of ether, of gangrene, to see barefoot fifteen-year-old boys armed to the teeth on a deserted road, what does it do to you, the noise the night the antiaircraft fire in the helicopter. Fear, death. Passport in his pocket. He's off again. French journalist. War reporter. Death brushes past him, blows on his neck, but she's more interested in other people. It could happen but it never does.

With him: kebabs in Barbès, the flea market in Saint-Ouen, army-navy surplus stores. Military clothing. I have forage caps, kepis, fatigues. I am extremely well informed about uniforms, armies, ranks. Present arms, attention, at ease. I'll go to Polytechnique if you want. Or I'll be Lord Jim. I listen to Bach. I don't know where I discovered Bach, my parents' tastes are more modern, but I'm obsessed with Bach.

I enter my mother's world, but my mother's world is not the world, it's her. Everyone does that with her. We watch her, we realize we've never seen anyone like her, we let ourselves be drawn in, we tell ourselves that nothing else exists but her. My mother inhales you, she swallows you up. You're in the belly of the whale. It's beautiful, it's hot, it's spectacular. You don't want anything different. My father is also like that, with her. He and I are like that, we look at her and try to understand what it is we're seeing. To be swallowed up by her is so good. Sometimes we can't bear it, so my father goes off to do some reporting, he goes to China, he disappears. I have asthma, I suffocate, at night most of all. Like Bacon, like Proust. The illness of geniuses. I spend my childhood with an inhaler in my pocket, a little blue dildo next to my thigh, my own little fix.

My mother at this time: an apartment a quiet life a husband a child a spaniel. And sunglasses boots coats and makeup which signal anything but ordinary life. You can't have a normal life when you have that face, that look. Always made-up. I hardly ever saw my mother without makeup. Very very rarely. Even at the end when she hid her terrible whiskey under her pillow.

Who could ask for a more perfect dealer than a Belgian princess, Fanchon van something or other? She had also been a model. Fanchon wasn't her real name. Aristocrats nickname each other after horses. When I think of the word *bohemian,* I think of Fanchon's apartment, dark and messy, clothes strewn on sofas, pillows, curtains, a theatrical atmosphere. *Malte Laurids Brigge* via Nan Goldin and Cookie Mueller. We stop in for five minutes after school. It's two minutes away, a little ways up the rue Saint-Jacques, across from the Musée de la Mer. They ask me to wait in one room, my mother goes off with Fanchon, comes back to get me. My sense of what's going on is vague, but I have a sense of it all the same, kids are not that dumb. Usually it's my dad who goes to see Fanchon, he calls, he says Can I come by, he goes, alone. Usually it's my dad who takes care of the drugs, he's been a junkie since he was twenty, that's what interests him in life. That and my mother. Even after her death. For years and years afterward. Drug addicts are strong, they're the opposite of weak, they're unstoppable. A knight's training.

They always fought. Whether or not I was there didn't change anything. He was the one who hit her, but it seemed to me, nevertheless, that she was the one who wanted violence, who *was* violence, she brought it out in him, a violence he hadn't previously known. Without her he was never violent. Never was after her, either. In no other phase of his life, no matter what happened, did I ever see him get angry. I never even saw him irritated. Even with the drinking, through the most difficult times, he never raised his voice. Gentle as a lamb. Gandhi. With her he became something else. He had access to something else. Maybe he was looking for his own violence, maybe he was happy to find it. That was between them. Like a hit of speed. Layered on top of opium, which made them sleep, and dampened everything. Sometimes the next day she'd have bruises on her face, a black eye, a split lip, it was like a hangover. They loved each other that way, since forever, since before I was born. It exhausted them. Sometimes she said she would leave him but they never left each other, of course they didn't.

I loved my father, I loved my mother, like everyone does. So what? I repeat: So what?

8

I'm only interested in what interests me. I made that decision five years ago. It's very easy. It's crazy how easy it is. That's its biggest advantage, the power of simplifying things. What interests me is existence itself, not the conditions of existence. For example whether I live in a studio near Montparnasse or in a tiny studio on the place de la Contrescarpe or at a friend's on the rue Chapon, or in a one bedroom on the boulevard de Clichy, or in a studio high in a tower in Arles, or that in the years before that I lived all over the place, or that sometimes I had no money at all, or that it's a little better now, these are things that don't matter at all. I could have a huge apartment, furniture, knickknacks, clothes, cash, none of that would matter. Whether I live here or there, whether the people I speak to are or are not the woman I love, what I'm reading, if I've slept well or badly, what I'm eating, it doesn't matter. Whatever happens I work, I swim, I see the woman I love or I see no one at all. It's organized. Slightly organized. If something new interests me, I can work it into my system. Ever since I started living this way, loads of interesting events have come to pass. By *events* I mean things that are meaningful with regard to my work or my life, which amounts to the same thing since my work is also existence itself. By *events* I'm thinking for instance of women. They turn up. They like me. If I like them too I go to bed with them. There's no misunderstanding. It's because I live like this that they turn up. So I go on. And when it doesn't work anymore I leave, or sometimes they do. It's the same with apartments. When I'm tired of living where I live, I leave. It's simple. I could easily live without an apartment just as I could easily live without a mistress. Life is a series of entrances and exits. I think that's what I mean by *events*. Entrances and exits. That's always interested me. In order for an entrance or an exit to happen, in order for it to be fluid, you have to stay light at your core. No agenda. No possessions. No opinions either, or not too many of them. To have as light a core as possible. Or even no core at all. My life is very simple now. That it all became possible through homosexuality doesn't have to distract us. No muss no fuss. The system doesn't allow for it.

9

In my family there are no factory workers, no farmers, no maids, no schoolteachers, no shopkeepers, no low-level civil servants, and also no convicts, whores, fags, murderers, no strangers, no refugees, no immigrants. In my family there are government ministers (under de Gaulle, Pétain, Giscard, Pompidou, Napoleon III, Louis XV, etc.), deputies (under each government), counts, barons, a duchess, two famous painters, a railway-station architect, a winner of the Prix de Rome, some rabbis, pastors, medical-school professors, diplomats, members of the Jockey Club and of the Académie Française. Aristocrats included, the bourgeoisie are ridiculous. They think they're important, they are ridiculous. If the bourgeois could see themselves, if people outside the bourgeoisie only knew. Ridiculous to the point that it should be outlawed. It is the grotesquerie of the bourgeoisie—of all the bourgeoisie since it's an infinitely large sample of the population—

which shapes the particular character of its violence, and makes it unbearable. It took me a while to understand that class violence had gone out of fashion, by which I mean the violence of the lower toward the upper classes. That of the upper toward the lower I know well, I know it intimately, from the inside. I spent my childhood watching people who make the law, how they know nothing about other people, how ugly they were, too. It's a symbol of their inelegance, the absence of self-questioning that plays out on the bodies, the faces, the clothing, the haircuts, everything visible. For instance in Paris on the Line 4 of the Métro you see it very clearly, how beauty and ugliness are distributed according to class, the beautiful people as the line runs south from Porte de Clignancourt to Strasbourg–Saint-Denis, and the empty ones who take over as the line becomes more bourgeois, from the Marais to the sixth, how the bourgeois doesn't really live in his body. I was struck by that when I was a child, the violence and the ugliness of the people who make the law, and later, of those who apply it. For a long time it was my job to decide what justice was, to see the judges doing their work, their work which consisted of putting poor people in prison, because the law is against the poor, because justice is against the poor, that's how it is and it can't be otherwise, because it's not even the judges' fault, that all that plays out on another level, one that is impossible to dismantle, I don't know, all I know is that to see all of that close up disgusted me. In the beginning you think being a lawyer means defending people, that it's to be in opposition, and then you come to see that it's about permissiveness, allowing the judges to do their own dirty work, allowing the law to be calmly crushing, that that is a lawyer's job, to legitimize violence, class violence from on high toward those below. The other kind—from those below toward those on high—seems to have disappeared. The poor rape and kill one another. So there you have it, what can be done for them? It's for these kinds of reasons that I stopped being a lawyer. Before I was disgusted, but now I don't care, I don't care about the poor, I don't care about the rich, I don't care about bourgeois or not bourgeois, I really, truly, deeply don't care, I can't even begin to tell you how much I don't care. C. is always crying at the sight of homeless people, she always gives them money; me, it's been a long time since I have given them anything, I don't even see them anymore, I have no more pity. As long as they don't come and bother me, come and bother me for money or a cigarette, Shut up, shut up do you hear me. One day I'm going to end up slapping the poor sod who comes to bother me. I don't care about the class struggle, I don't care about the poor, or about my ancestors who were ministers or artists, it's all the same to me. Shut up. Shut up do you hear me. Whoever you are, shut up.

10

Every summer we visit my mother's château in the Basque
Country. My mother suntans on the roof. We swim in the
freezing-cold Nive when it gets too hot. I watch her and
her sisters dive in from the trees. They are like animals,
with their thin muscled tense brown bodies. They are
always fighting. It always seems like they might kill each
other. The men are the husbands, they're not part of it.
They aren't the power, the violence, the beauty, their
bodies are fragile and white. One night in the large
kitchen things get more heated than usual, I look at the
knives on the table at the height of my eyes, I wonder
when they will see them too and grab hold of them and go
all the way with their violence which is so much like the
essence of Violence it strikes me as normal, coherent with
their own essence, I don't see any disconnect. But no,
amid the screams and insults one of them turns her
back and leaves through the service stairway, and then

everything calms down. Back to afternoon naps under the cedar, my mother tanning on the roof, the Nive, dinners at which the adults are beautiful. My summer life there is a beret, espadrilles, the park, the old horses, the pediment of the castle, and the boys from the village who are better at pelota ball than I am, because they live here year-round. I don't know if they look at me weird because of the château or because I'm a girl, or because of the way I have of being a girl. All summer I piss standing up like a boy, I go see the horses in the morning, I try to play pelota ball, I learn to ride a bike, I ride horseback behind my mother, I feed ducks in a stinky barn. One day I will leave, but for now I'm in training. That's what I'm doing, when I cycle, when I build forts, when I learn English, when I read stories about heroes. I spend my whole childhood training and waiting.

The château burned when I was five, it caught fire one night, it was like a death in the family, I was already used to those. A fire is always good in the absence of a revolution. In any case my mother couldn't bear her family any longer. She had to rid herself of them. We stopped going to the Basque Country and started going to Touraine, to see my father's parents. They strike me as resembling less the Guermantes than the Verdurins. Of course I've read Proust, I've read all the books, coming from my family, with my personality, given what I'm doing today, nothing less than full-time writing, which is the only important thing, but Proust will die soon, he has to die, Proust and all the others, all books perhaps, maybe it's urgent that all literature die, literature which offers us the world, which has turned into its opposite, into the bourgeoisie itself, its bulwark, its reward, its justification, just as the Church has become the opposite of Christ, who was poverty, the religion of the poor and of pure love, and not of the powerful, literature has to die, perhaps, to rebecome that furtive thing, a job for roaches, the language of rats, and not this hideous thing, this cultural artifact, as repugnant as other cultural artifacts. Books have nothing to do with culture, they contain things that are far more important than culture, things that are not beautiful or spectacular, or amusing, or tasteful, or of their time, or having to do with questions of historical moment and debates and ideas—just this ratlike, roach-like thing, what is absolutely solitary in life, maybe writers should return to what they are, to what I am, a roach, a rat. They ought to write what they alone understand. What they've seen and understood. To write as if they don't understand anything. Or maybe they should just keep quiet. Maybe books, too, have become obscene.

Montlouis is the Verdurins' Touraine, and my cousins are there. Often my uncles and aunts as well. My parents stay in a room in some distant wing or in a small house which is separate from the main house. Often they don't come down to eat, they don't show up at the table. My mother wears sunglasses; my dad returns to Paris as soon as he can. They're bored. It's clear they can only be bored with these people, with these brothers and their wives, with my grandfather the prime minister. Obviously there's nothing else to do but be bored, faced with the casseroles the applesauce the soup and the rib steaks, so dull is this lifestyle, the turns of phrase that go with it, that it makes you want to send the plates flying, to tell them where they can stick their entrecôte and their politicians and their canned commentary on France and this fake family and all their fake words. With these people who have no bodies. With Grandpa the prime minister who doesn't have a body, who's nothing but his ugly tie and his title of prime minister, his name and the stories he tells himself that everyone buys. With his sons who hide their bodies behind empty sentences, who hide their fears behind their marriages, the correct number of children, and their adequate careers, everything that isn't real. These daddy's boys who want nothing else but to be the favorite son, who rope everyone else—wives and children alike—into the family business of being called Debré. It's their life's work. It's maybe not their fault, maybe they haven't read anything, maybe they don't realize that names don't exist. All those who doubt it are their enemies. In life it's either beauty or power. Power is for those who lack the courage to be beautiful. The two sides are at war, since forever, since the *Iliad* and the *Odyssey*. You only need to place them side by side to see that they don't get on. That they have nothing to say to one another. My uncles and aunts didn't like my parents and vice versa. They stared at each other, mute. Through his indifference, without saying a word, my father had denounced their system. My mother provokes them with her beauty, her milieu, her class. She says nothing, she is polite, but her disdain for them seeps through her pores. Of everyone in the house she prefers the servants.

Every family invents and feeds its own madness, because it can't survive without it. The bourgeoisie are no less mad than the aristocrats. They are mad, of course they are, the Debrés, their madness is called the State, they call it *la France*. To forget, perhaps, that they're a little bit Jewish. He's forgotten he bears a Jewish name, Grandpa the prime minister, that his grandfather was a rabbi, that he has cousins who never returned from the camps. Things might have been different if instead of Debré he had been called Blum or Aron, then it would have been more difficult to forget that they were Jews. Debré doesn't sound Jewish, and if you don't know you don't know, so they pretended they didn't know. It was easier that way, since they believed they had to be French, and to be French, you have to not be Jewish. There is a lie at the heart of their love for France, in their obsession with France, the eternal France from the *Song of Roland* to Charles Péguy via Racine and Barrès, universal France, Jacobin France, where you are French and nothing else, not Breton not Alsatian, not rich or poor, not Jewish, there is a mania in this France and they all believe in it, they wrote it themselves with their laws and their constitution. A mania or a lie, shame, hatred for the Jew within. What does it mean to them, to be Jewish? What impurity do they see there? What stain? It's like a latent homosexuality or a class complex. Purity is France. They are against Israel. They never talk about the Holocaust. That's a thing that never existed. There was the war and they talk about that a lot. There were resistance fighters and collaborators, Germans and Allies, and where were the Jews in all this? They never talk about it. The Alsatian cousins who didn't come back, we never talk about them. Their religion is the France of the Recueil Lebon, the kings of France, the great laws of the Third Republic. The rest doesn't exist. The rabbis of Westhoffen don't exist.

11

Insanity everywhere, nonstop delirium. You have only to listen to the adults, the way they go on and on and never stop talking, and the silence of their children, who are embarrassed by them, by their mother, by their father, by all the others. All you have to do is go outside, to the parks, to the school gates, go idle in the streets, they're heaving with hysterical parents and uncomfortable children. And silent children. Children who keep quiet. They have understood that the one thing that is truly forbidden is to tell adults to shut up, even though it's the most important thing, the healthiest thing. When such a thing does come to pass, say in adolescence, they chalk it up to teenage angst, they say it will pass, instead of listening. Instead of shutting up and being ashamed, we yell at them as if they were the ones who needed to be punished, we take them to therapists as if they were the ones who needed help. Children are trained to love the insane, to obey the deranged, to say their lines in the idiotic play that is child-hood told to children, performed by families for other families, by parents for other parents, by mothers, by fathers, by everyone for everyone. The bourgeoisie tells its own story, and school as well, with its microviolence that is excellent preparation for that which will come later, all the domestic violence which must be accepted and everyone protects. Incest and hitting are off-limits; every-thing else is OK, the law says so, article 111-4 of the Code pénal, *criminal law must be interpreted strictly*. How much are you willing to withstand? That's what we ought to ask newborns, before we give them a name.

Names are like Pokémon cards, they come with points. You lose points or you gain them. In the war of names, my father's family wins out over my mother's. The name of my father, my grandfather, my great-grandfather—that is to say, my name—wins out over many names. France, the State, politics, medicine, and even a little bit of the arts, that's them, that's us. That's the story they tell, that they tell me, that other people have told me, because other people believe it too. My name even turns up in the names of streets and on the sides of buildings, I see it with my own eyes and the lady who does the prerecorded announcements on public transport reminds me of it, in case I'd like to get off at the next station which has the same name as I do. Their obsession with their own names (my *own* name, I who own nothing, my family name, I who no longer have a family) is like a talisman to ward off death, their protection from all instability, for the bourgeoisie are scared, that's what other people don't often see, the immense fear of the bourgeoisie. I too have a place in this story of a name. Early on people looked askance at me, with my angry silence and my boys' clothes, they took me aside, they asked me why. But as I got older, and racked up the accolades, and the good school, and law school, and more accolades, and the bar, and all my bourgeois little achievements, they liked me better, of course. I could have been the perfect heir to the name. Or rather, I was the only heir. It wasn't my sister or any of my cousins, everyone knew it and I did too. I could have been like them, I could have given in. I'd rather die. R.A.T.H.E.R. D.I.E., I had it tattooed on my neck. C. doesn't like it but it helps me keep to my system. Of course I'm their heir, of course I disinherit them.

I said that I didn't care about everything else but that's not true. The truth is I'm the opposite of someone who doesn't care. Everything I do is because I care. When I leave a woman, it's because I don't love her and because we don't have the right to lie about love. If I'm no longer a lawyer, it's because I had something more important to do, namely writing my books. The point of my books is to explain what's happening, it's not to tell the story of my life, it's to explain what's happening and how we should live. My books are something I do against that miserable life, that's all, the miserable life I saw, that I see all around me. It seems important to say that to people. That we speak of that miserable life. It seems important to question that life, to really have at it, rather than defend the poor, who in any case are just going to go to prison, because that's how things are, because justice is the result of a thousand consequences and it's pointless to try to deal with the consequences of consequences, it's better to accept the root causes. So seeing as how I'm not trying to start a revolution, I'm writing books. But I want to be read correctly, I don't want to be told to be nice, to make as if I were a nice girl, polite, to be told that I have to pay attention to what I say, that I shouldn't give people the impression that I'm spitting in their faces, when that's exactly what people need, to have their faces spat at, to have someone explain to them that enough is enough, life is miserable, that this miserable life is killing them, because this miserable life is killing everyone. People aren't serious. They're not serious about their bodies. They're not serious about their work. They're not serious about their desires. They're not serious about love. They're not serious about what they think. They're not serious about themselves. They don't see things through, right through to the end. They only go halfway. It's not easy to see things through. You have to be serious. You have to try. Now I've chosen, I've been choosing for years and everything has become very simple, even when it's not going well, who cares about happiness, happiness doesn't exist, there's a superior ideal, it's moral and it's practical, what counts is to have chosen it, what counts is the decision. After that everything is simple, that's the way I do things now. But you, what do you want, what do you choose, what kind of life, which camp, because you can't not choose, you can't just leave it up to fate, to the elements, to habit, to other people, to exterior powers. This miserable life is my obsession, I've been thinking about it since I was born, I've built up a body of knowledge against it. I am not describing my feelings here—emotions and feelings are repugnant—but my ideas, my ideas against this miserable life. If I live the way I do, if I write the way I do, it's not for me, it's not out of personal preference, personal preference is a minuscule thing. Good taste, bad taste, taste is the degree zero of thought, to approach things through the question of taste is to abandon the question of morality, the only one that matters. It began with Barthes, all of this, with his nit-picking, typical of the intellectual bourgeoisie but useless, powerless, melancholic, pretentious, moribund, deathly, bourgeois literature written for the bourgeoisie, literature that wants nothing to change. But Barthes will also fade away and let me just say that I prefer Proust. Proust is the opposite of powerlessness. Proust was out of his mind at least, and didn't apologize for it. No, if I live the way I do it's not for my own personal comfort, it's a position I have taken with regard to the order of things, it's because I have to do what I do, otherwise the world would be insane. That's what I think, that I am preserving the sanity of the world with my life. If I live as I do, if I write as I do, it's because at some point somebody has to, we can't go on with the slight obscenity of the bourgeoisie and the family and of childhood, which is all the same obscenity, because these three things—the family, childhood, and the bourgeoisie—hold hands on this infernal merry-go-round on which we find ourselves imprisoned, which they spoon-feed us every day in books, in magazines, at the therapist's office, in the judge's chambers, in our photo IDs, the madness is everywhere. The unbearable thrumming of idiocy and violence and ugliness. Obscenity is all the rage, since we've had no more revolutions, since we've had to accept the world as it is, no longer take up arms, kill our fathers and mothers, turn power on its head, assassinate the powerful, since we've been told that war isn't reasonable, that no one is your enemy, that we should just stay home, waiting for death, no more struggling, time to be happy. What I think is that nobody is only one person, that each of us is the instrument of something else in the overall balance of the world, a side to choose in the war of everyone against everyone else, of justice against injustice, of good against evil. Yes: I live and write against the obscenity of this miserable life. Living any other way would make me vomit, would make me ashamed, it would be to dress as so many others do, to read the miserable books people read, to live as they live, to see a therapist to help me put up with it, to get drunk to put up with it, buy things to put up with it. Not to put up with it but to put up with it anyway, that would make me crazy. Everything must be refused. Refuse everything it is possible to refuse in this miserable life, do not consent, do not bear the unbearable. If I refuse, if I betray, it's to fight this obscenity. I betray my origins on principle, as a point of departure for everything else. Origins should always be betrayed. To accept them is to compromise; give in that very first time and all the other times are made possible. It's the primal act of complicity, of cowardliness, the first humiliation too. Whereas refusing origins is the first interruption; it then becomes possible to go on refusing. We have to learn to refuse, to betray everything we're asked to accept about this obscene world, which I betray as I've done a thousand times, as I would do again. I commit these acts of betrayal to remember what there is when there is nothing. I betray my origins to prove that the world is founded on a lie, that everything has to be reinvented, but that before that it all has to be destroyed. If we want to be able to look at ourselves in the mirror before we die, everything has to be rinsed with acid, gasoline, and fire. To have done that.

12

My sister called. We haven't really spoken for years. She's pregnant with her third, they've left the city and moved to Touraine, not far from my father's house, she's put her daughters in a private school, she has a dog, a house, a 4x4, a lawyer husband who has a beard, a motorcycle, a château. We have nothing to talk about, and that's basically why we don't speak. That she is my sister changes nothing. What could I say to her, when she believes in things I don't? She believes in childhood, in marvelous, tragic parents, she believes that until the day you die you are your parents' child, your children's mother, your husband's wife. Things that do not exist for me. Things which are lies, for me. Things we tell ourselves to keep from thinking. She told me about my father, the tumors in his lungs, the metastasis in his liver and in a bone, she doesn't know which one. She says he'll see the doctor on Monday, that they'll do a spinal tap to see what can be done for him. She says the doctor couldn't tell her how much time he has left, she cries, I don't say anything. She tells me He was doing well when you were there, that it would be good if I went back, I hadn't thought we'd said very much to one another when I was there, two months ago, when I spent a few weeks with him, I thought he was dying back then, that I was witnessing it, he was telling me, so I didn't tell him it wasn't true. He watched series to distract himself from his impending death, that was a new thing, the series, that's what he did all day, it seemed to be working, I told myself series are useful when you're dying. I bought him frozen Bounty bars and frozen Snickers bars when I went to the supermarket, that was all I could find, they interested him more than whatever I had to say, and in any case I didn't say much, nor did he, we didn't talk, we don't really love each other, my father and I, what can you do, there's nothing to be done, it was easier to buy him frozen Bounty bars and Snickers bars than to talk to him, and for him to say thanks and to eat them than to answer me, I thought it was always something else when things like death were on the horizon, I thought that death wasn't the problem, it was what needed to be done to get there, all the steps. I thought it was weird that my sister was crying, I thought maybe she had arranged her life that way, telling herself that the people who mattered were her father her husband and her children, without asking too many questions, because they were there, because that's how things were, I thought it was too easy to call that love, what occurs between you and the people around you, I thought it was a way of avoiding the question of love, I thought my father and I stopped loving each other long ago, something I had realized two months earlier, each of us in opposite corners of the house, not speaking because we had nothing to say. I thought that made sense because my childhood had ended a long time ago, that it had been a long time since he'd known anything about my life, since he'd wanted to know anything for that matter, that his life consisted of watching series or television and that's it, that he was no longer interested in me or my sister, that I knew very well that he cared about my sister as little as he cared about me, I knew he didn't give a shit about her just as he didn't give a shit about me. I thought that I didn't think about him or his death anymore either, just like he no longer thought about me, about my life, that it was logical, that it was right, that I think more about whomever I'm hanging out with, whichever girl I'm seeing, than my father, my dead mother, my sister, my twelve-year-old son whom I haven't seen in four years. I thought that family had completely disappeared from my life, I thought it wasn't sad or serious, I thought it was normal, that it was even healthy to think about things this way, I thought that if you don't see people they eventually fade away, and that father mother child it doesn't mean very much if they're not there, except for people who want to believe it does, and the majority of people do, but I had always been this way, and no doubt my father as well, only having faith in concrete realities, in established fact, and in a concrete sense family had disappeared from my reality, it had become a word emptied of all material fact, of all substance, proving that the word itself was empty because it could be emptied. I thought this unintentional experiment, this series of accidents in my life all pointed to the extinction of the family, had helped me attain a kind of modernity of thought and existence, that it was something I had managed to do, that I had proved, which had been proved inside of me, that I was proof personified given the absence of family in my life, although I still had a father a son a sister, although they weren't even dead, and we lived in the same country, the same city, sometimes the same neighborhood; that we lived in the same temporal space, that I was me, Constance Debré, proof personified that family is only an illusion, just as Galileo proved that the sun which appeared to rotate around the earth was also an illusion, that it was good to be proof personified of the fallacious character of an intellectual hypothesis, to demonstrate the falsity of banal things, to prove that they are only beliefs, not reality, like religion, Marxism, capitalism, or psychoanalysis, like all the systems of thought in which we might choose to believe, that we can choose to follow without the slightest material proof of their veracity, and that consequently we can decide not to believe in them, not to follow them. I thought it was good to draw near to the truth, that I saw nothing to be sad about, or to disagree with, or to find tragic, that I found that it was always better than to tell yourself stories about people who don't like you and whom you don't like. I asked myself if my readers would say to themselves Yes, it's true, the family doesn't exist, if they would stop pretending to love and to suffer from loving so badly, I asked myself what the world would look like if people stopped lying to themselves about love, if they let go of false loves and therefore began to love with more force, with more vitality, increase in quantity and in quality. I thought as well of all those I had loved and lost, I thought it was always good to love the most amount of people possible in a life, I thought that family, the love of family, faith in family, in fact it was only fear of asking questions about love, and that, on the question of love, I believed as much in quantity as in quality, in fact they were not opposed to one another, I thought that what was courageous in love asked as often the question of quantity as of quality, that I didn't trust people who always opposed quantity and quality, I thought of all the people I had loved, of the women especially whom I had loved for the past five years, as opposed to very few men before that, except for the twenty years with P. of course, I thought that while I had never had a particular knack for loss, by chance and then by training, if I hadn't gritted my teeth a thousand times, I would not have loved so many people over the course of my life, I have asked myself how many more people I will love, what their names will be, their bodies, their stories, what they are going to teach me, how we will love each other, touch and seduce each other, wound each other, leave each other, I thought deep down that we have the lives we want to lead, or rather that we always manage a way to get our lives to resemble some ideal which must have imprinted itself somewhere in our cerebral cortex and that in my case it must take the form of something torn, stained, as threadbare as an old pair of jeans, that it was always the most beat-up versions that pleased me the most, that everything was as perfect as it had ever been, that reality is always perfect.

13

Little bottles of neon yellow liquid, the scent of pastis. Paregoric elixir, or tincture of opium, it sounds like something out of *César Birotteau*. You can buy it over the counter. The instructions say it's to be used to soothe stomachache. All the junkies take it when they need a fix. Burroughs writes about it, and even Joyce in *Ulysses*. Over the counter, that means even kids can buy it at the end of the '70s, beginning of the '80s. In the countryside, when I go to the village on my bike to buy fishing hooks or Mammoth Rouge firecrackers, which smell like gunpowder when they explode, I stop in at the pharmacy for them. Bonjour madame, two bottles of paregoric elixir please. It's important to be polite. In theory you're meant to take it in small, diluted doses, it's measured in teaspoons, according to the instructions. They crack open the metal cap, they drink the bottle in one go, they grimace, I smell the odor. They also put paregoric elixir in my sister's baby bottle when she was born to wean her from the opium that my mother smoked when she was pregnant. My sister is a beautiful baby, with no apparent issues.

All that in full view of the others, in the middle of the others I should say, since it's in the countryside especially, far from their dealer, that they need these bottles. Maybe also in Paris, on days when they can't get their fix, but they muddle through, I'm not sure how. The countryside in question is Grandpa prime minister's, it's his town hall, it's my father's brothers who vie with one another to become a minister like Grandpa, it's the sisters-in-law who have their own roles to perform, it's the nice cousins I play tennis with, it's my grandfather who speaks of France in exalted tones and who goes to work in his office with letterhead for each ministry he's led, it's my uncles who will end up being ministers like Daddy, right-wing like Daddy. The ultimate humiliation is to be the one who doesn't inherit Daddy's constituency, that's how far gone they are in worshipping him. Maybe it excites him, Grandpa the prime minister, to see his litter of puppies fighting over who will be the best son. Each suffers from the others' successes—such are the wounds of grown men. My father has always been the bad son, because he doesn't give a shit about the minister. I often go into my grandfather's office when he isn't there, a place where no one comes to find me, where I can be alone. I can be alone there for hours, I sit down at the desk, I open drawers, I help myself to some paper, Minister of Defense, Minister of the Interior, Minister of Justice, I write letters, I give orders, I command troops, I govern.

Sometimes in the morning, en route to catch the bus to school, in front of the pharmacy of Le Drugstore on boulevard Saint-Germain which is open until two o'clock in the morning, I pick up the empty bottles of paregoric elixir and empty blister packs of Néo-codion. I know it was junkies in need of a hit who drank the bottles, swallowed the tablets quick as they could, to trick their bodies, to sleep a little before sunrise, to hang on til they could meet their dealer. It's always nice to know things other people don't. After the public school on the rue Saint-Jacques, I go to Henri-IV, the crème de la crème, professors' kids who will go on to ENS as long as they do everything they're told, good kids who love their teachers, who are bored during vacation. I have nothing to say to them either. I'm waiting for it all to end—childhood, school, parents.

14

Opium is decadent, but bourgeois. Opium is: ambassadors, writers, filmmakers, journalists, pretty women, big apartments, travel, books, it's a perfume by Saint Laurent that my mother wears (clearly as a joke). It's the '70s, it's a vanished world. Saigon has fallen, Asia has become communist, little by little opium is harder to get out, and they make less and less of it. Twice my father has had to go to Laos to find some. He switches hotels, he shakes off the police, he lays traps, the mountains, a village, a transaction, returns to Chiang Mai, opium in the film cans that he mails to the post office that's holding his mail, takes a 747 to Roissy–Charles de Gaulle, and gets his drugs in Paris. It would be *Midnight Express* if he were caught. He does it once. He does it twice. He stops. He changes drugs. Welcome to the '80s, to the world of heroin, the great equalizer, more effective than unemployment, than Mitterrand.

New friends, new junkies. The heroin crew. I prefer them to the opium lot. Younger less bougie more beat-up. They're hustlers. They're clever. They're not as slick. Usually they sniff, sometimes they shoot up. Like Flo. First she was HIV positive. Then she had AIDS. Then she died. She lived with her mother and her fatherless daughter. I see her daughter a bit. She comes with us to Touraine one summer. She's the same age as me. I don't like her, Sarah is her name, she has too much of an unhappy air about her.

My father loses his job on TV, he's too wasted, we lose the apartment. They live in hotels. Rue de Buci, rue de Seine. Small local hotels. The Louisiane, etc. For six months I live with my grandparents on the rue Jacob. With my sister who goes to preschool. My parents come by in the morning and the evening for school homework dinner. I love my grandmother, I ignore Grandpa the prime minister, he's disgusted me for a while.

No more pipes in the evening. Now it's powder in little folded bits of white paper. It's a silver box in my mother's handbag. It's the straws she cuts up. Striped red or blue on white plastic. Lines she traces with little pocket-knives, with handles made of horn or ivory. Sometimes she has a little powder under her nose. I indicate it to her. And then the bags under her eyes, the gray complexion, the sunglasses. Her absence. Her falling asleep. The cigarettes that fall. That burn the sheets, the books. My parents' books are all burned.

She's stoned in the middle of nowhere. I keep watch over her. Her eyes close, her chin falls. Maman! She wakes up, sits up. Quoi ça? she asks, in a thick voice. Maybe she's trying to say What's that, maybe English is coming back to her when she's high. Heroin then pills. Alcohol came later. When there was no money left for anything.

I'm in sixth grade, then seventh. I hate school. When they called me after the bac to attend *hypokhâgne*,[1] I said No thank you. No more Henri-IV. No *hypokhâgne*. No more grubby classrooms with grubby teachers.

Next my parents rent a flat on the rue Bonaparte. All four of us are together again. It's just above the Petit Saint-Benoît, an old neighborhood restaurant. French food. Red-and-white-checkered paper napkins. Pitcher of wine. Leeks vinaigrette. Hard-boiled eggs with mayo. Duras goes there. Never ran into her. Yann Andréa, yes. But later, at the Flore. Looking lost. We stayed two years. Evicted. They stopped paying the rent. Alcohol during this period, and pills. The worst combination. They're letting go. That's all you can say, really, they're letting go. My

---

1. A rigorous two-year academic preparation program undertaken after high school in preparation for the École normale supérieure entrance exam.

father doesn't really have a job. No more reportages. He's writing screenplays for television, a little. Police procedurals, episodes of *Les cinq dernières minutes* with Commissioner Cabrol and Detective Ménardeau, slipping in beautiful women and plotlines about drugs. Sometimes for dinner we bring up croque monsieurs from the Pré aux Clercs, the café downstairs, or we get a folded crepe in a paper wrapper at the crepe stand on the rue Bonaparte.

I don't know if my sister can tell what's going on. Even I don't understand, at the beginning. What they tell us doesn't make sense. Especially her. He gets high too, of course he does, but we don't see it as much, he hides out in the living room which is his office which is his bedroom, he sleeps on the couch, they no longer sleep together. My sister and I are always with her, she's the one we see, the way she gets high, in her bedroom with the TV on, at the café, in the street, in the car.

I am in my grandfather's study on the rue Jacob. I have a private math lesson today. It's a dark room that looks out on the back of the garden. You can see the Temple of Friendship. Three fake-antique columns, Directoire- or revolutionary Freemason–style. That kind of bad taste. Inside, there are my grandfather's old papers, a French flag, *bleu blanc rouge*, the smell of damp. My grandparents' home used to belong to Natalie Barney. Colette, Proust,

Joyce, they all passed through. It's not the kind of world my grandparents like. My mother is the one who told me about Natalie Barney, who told me who she was, a poetess, a rich American heiress, a lesbian, the younger mistress of Liane de Pougy, and many others after that. She likes this story, my mother likes lesbians. She says she tried it once, with Simone, I know Simone, we run into her sometimes in the neighborhood, she lives with a woman, Etel, I look at Simone, my mother says she tried it but no, I don't know if it's true. She says she loved women when she was at boarding school, that it was normal. She tells me all of this, she tells me that if I am a lesbian, if that's what I'm into, with my boys' clothes, that it's no big deal. That I shouldn't hide it from myself, that's all. With my mother we sometimes go to the Vieux Casque, a tiny restaurant at the bottom of the rue Bonaparte, toward the rue Visconti, just a few tables at the top of a stairway, the owner is a lesbian. I spent a lot of time in cafés and restaurants when I was a child, even when we didn't have any money, even with my parents' bad checks, neighborhood joints or the local Chinese, nothing fancy, I think it was an act of resistance against dining rooms, grocery stores, pots and pans, against the stomach, the stomach as valued more than the brain, than the heart, against everything that turns to shit. The Vieux Casque was always festive, because the place was tiny, because they only served two or three simple dishes, they played old records that sounded like Berlin in the '20s, because it was like an old shack, a little dark with old lamps, because of the family atmosphere, a weird family, the way we'd have liked family to be. The way the patronne gazed at my mother, my mother's gaze. She says they met twenty years before in a girls' nightclub, my mother says she liked going there. The waiters were young, beautiful, always gay, sometimes they got sick, sometimes they died.

Rue Jacob is decorated in bourgeois tones of ugly: beige and brown, nineteenth-century paintings, Louis Philippe furniture. The bourgeoisie do not love beauty, they mistrust it. *Bourgeois* means pathetic, it means fearful, it means ashamed, it means everything it's crucial not to be. My mother teaches me this. Aristocrats are crazy, but not about everything. There is a garden there. Useful for dogs, for playing soccer with my cousins, for parking my grand-mother's metallic-beige Renault 5. My grandfather is still an MP. He goes to the Assemblée nationale. He's writing his memoirs. I have never read them. Nobody cares. In the right-hand drawer of the roll-top desk there are Dupont pens and double-sided pencils (red and blue); in the middle drawer, Assemblée nationale letterhead, I take some for scrap paper. The student who is tutoring me arrives on his bicycle. One day my parents are there, they're fighting, the student doesn't say anything, neither do I, we're concentrated on our work, we pretend not to hear. The fighting gets louder, I stare at the equation, I don't see it anymore. They're in the kitchen next door, she's screaming, I leave the study, my father has a knife, they see me, they calm down, I go back into the study, I finish my math lesson. When I walk my tutor out to his bike in the courtyard, he opens his satchel and fastens it around the bar of the frame. I would like to do that one day. And to have a boy's bike because I will be a boy.

My grandmother died in Natalie Barney's bedroom, a long time after. The immense bedroom above the garden. There were two single beds there, one for him, one for her. He died a few years earlier, one summer at Montlouis. His final years were not great, with the wheelchair, the nurses, the Parkinson's. He stopped talking. Hatred surfaced against him. He couldn't fight back. Hatred or, rather, indifference. All of a sudden people stopped caring about him. The most shocking was my father who was very kind to him, though he had hated him his whole life. Every evening he stopped by the rue Jacob to help my grandmother get him to bed, it took hours. Every evening, for years. The other brothers could care less, they were ministers, they were busy.

A color Polaroid. A sex pic, as they would say today. A slightly shabby hotel room. Her, at night. One lamp. Dark furniture. It looks dirty. Ugly colors. She's wearing stockings. We can see the tops of them, the transition to nude skin on her skinny thighs. Thinner than before. She's leaning on a dresser. She's looking at him. She's posing.

She's not smiling. It's sexual and sinister. Thanatos rather than Eros. Otto Dix, Ingrid Thulin in *Les damnés*. When did I see this photograph? Where and when? Among her belongings? Or after her death, with his own things? Did he jerk off to it? Can you do that with a dead body? It's better than *greatly missed* or *mother of my children*. Better than two people who have outlived their desire for one another.

They stop paying rent on the place on the rue Bonaparte, the electricity as well, which frequently gets turned off. Again they lose the apartment. Again we have to move. We land behind Montparnasse in a sort of HLM.[2] I still hate school. I cut class as much as possible. I tell people I have asthma, which, moreover, is true. I don't see anyone, I don't go to parties, I want to join the army, I build models, I yell at my mother.

We have no money left at all, everything is difficult, grocery shopping and everything else, the bailiffs come, it's not abject misery but we're struggling. Sometimes my mother talks about one of her ex-boyfriends, she says she's going to see him, that she has a date, that she's going to run away. She's started spouting nonsense, junkies are always lying. My father is never there, or he's in his bedroom with the shutters closed, bottles under the bed. My

2. *Habitation à loyer modéré* (public housing).

mother has moved into the living room, that's where she sleeps and watches TV. My mother referred to her mother as PPLH, Passera-Pas-L'Hiver (Won't Last the Winter), thinking she was in for a small inheritance, but she dies before my grandmother.

I yell at my mother. I'm the only one left to do it. Someone has to be in charge of being angry. I come home from school, I examine her, eyes, appearance, voice, clothes, smell. All it takes is one look to see. She's been drinking. She drinks whiskey. Maybe the alcohol began with little flasks in her bag. She's always had enormous bags. Black leather. Then bottles. In the HLM days she'd say she was taking the dogs for a walk, the dogs had already been walked, the dogs don't need to piss, I say nothing, I go to the window, I confirm what I already know, she goes to the Chinese restaurant across the street, she buys her whiskey, she comes back upstairs, I say nothing to her, it's what, eight o'clock, ten o'clock in the morning. She hides her bottles all around her. In her bag, in her bed. At the café she orders whiskey and Coke. She orders them directly from the bar with our Cokes, mine and my sister's, she says hers is Coke too. As if I can't tell that it's not the same color. As if I couldn't smell it. The smell of her alcoholic's skin. You've been drinking, I tell her when I come home from school. She denies it, her voice thick, her gaze unsteady. During those years I asked the same question again and again. It's not a question. It's not a complaint either. I'm as tall as she is, and then I get taller. Now we face off, our bodies tense with conflict, and my sister cries like I used to, when our parents fought. I don't hit her but I understand. It did me good when this whole thing with my mother came to an end. The dead can help the living, too.

Aside perhaps from war, death, violence, work, and love, life is astonishingly unserious. It can make you crazy how unserious most things in life are. Whereas drugs, yes, drugs are serious, they make people serious. They create their own laws, and people who must submit to them. A junkie is an incredibly moral person. Having junkies for parents makes you grow up within a strong moral system. My luck was not to have been born into a family of ministers, no, my real lucky break, the one everyone should be jealous of, is having junkies for parents and a dead mother.

Maybe addicts can save nonaddicts, like the poor save the rich, and the believers the unbelievers. Maybe that's their job, their destiny in the overall balance of the world, maybe it demands sacrifice, on some obscure level of truth.

It seems as though I hardly ever see my father during this period, until the morning when I run into him on my way home from school, in front of the building we live in behind Montparnasse. He tells me she passed out, that she's in the hospital, that I should go to my grandparents', that he'll come by later. At first I think this is a good thing, that she will finally get the treatment she needs. But on the bus I realize I am experiencing the death of my mother, while Paris slides by behind the windows, unchanging, that death is something like that. During this period my father returns, we are reunited, during the months and years that follow, we live through them the three of us together, he, my sister, and I, in another apartment, again on the rue Bonaparte. Then we separate once more, I leave home, he goes to Sainte-Anne, my sister to a studio apartment, she's still in school. Then he has a series of studios, then he crashes here and there, and then he moves to Touraine. After my mother's death, it's his own way of falling apart, a slow-motion breakdown, endless, sometimes calm, and sometimes not. Years of going from one hospital to another, all across France, in rehab then in postrehab. Of getting used to all that, which gives shape to the years like the seasons. Of hearing the doctors say that he'd had a close call, that he should have died years ago, of getting used to him not dying, of getting used to it not ending. When I'm with him sometimes it seems like we are very alike in our mannerisms, our way of walking, talking, even of eating. I also hate sitting down at the table, I also prefer to eat alone, I also eat like a junkie, standing in the street or in front of the fridge, with a blend of obsession and not caring. It scares me to see our similarities when I get too close, but nobody else sees them because nobody comes to see him, because nobody sees us together. Maybe I'd feel the same way if my mother were still alive. At the very thought a chill goes over me. The idea that she might not be dead. My father has cancer of the tongue now. That and an oxygen machine, and a pacemaker, and Parkinson's, and the Subutex that he's taken for years like a good junkie. And the lungs that are going to give out eventually.

15

A second-rate commercial port near Perpignan. Cargo under the windows, the noise of the cranes, unloading the containers at night. In the living room there is a poster that reads *I Want to Believe* below a flying saucer. The lockdown is convenient for people like me, we barely notice it, or if we do it amuses us, it means there's more chances of having a fling. People like me appreciate minor catastrophes because they give the world a philosophical atmosphere. I said OK to this girl I've only seen twice, one afternoon in Saint-Étienne and one night in Paris. I put the computer in a bag with a pair of jeans and two T-shirts and I walked out of my room in the fourteenth. I'm trying, I'm always trying, I'm a *chevalier de la foi*, and every time I really believe. We work during the daytime. A. paints, I write. A. gives me a bed in the studio. We have sex in the afternoons. At night we sleep, each in our own room. A. went to see a shaman in the Amazon. A. visited

Area 51 in Roswell, New Mexico, or close by anyway. A. talks about the end of the world, A. says that since she was a child she's had a dream about the end of the world, which always picks up at the place it left off. A. says there's another world behind the world we see. A. has green eyes like fire and ice, I think that's why I'm here, and because of the *X-Files* poster in the living room. A. says that she's a girl, but she uses masculine pronouns, often but not always, she's given herself a boy's name, she says she doesn't care, or he doesn't care, that it's not important for her or him, but it's important to have balls to be a girl, sexy like Félix Maritaud, I sometimes say. She says that I'm not really a girl either. She says I'm her man, her girl, that she loves. She says when we sleep together we're neither girls nor boys, that we fuck differently. She says that she wanted pictures of my hand on her sex, that she would give me a tattoo when the lockdown was over, that a tattoo makes you vulnerable, that you have to learn to wait. We never did the photo or the tattoo. I stayed six weeks and then I left. If I didn't love her anymore, not enough, or not at all, what could she do, what could I do. The morning I told her, the day before my train, she took the Polo, she drove to the Lidl, she bought grapefruit liquor and a bottle of rosé, she said that's what they drink at her father's place in Vesoul, she sat by the window and drank and smoked, I was the bad guy or the good guy, I don't know which, there wasn't much to say. I checked the box labelled *important family reason* on the permission slip you needed to leave the house, I took a taxi and then some trains, there was no problem, I thought It's not that difficult to travel during the lockdown, I stayed in Paris for one night, in my 140 square feet in the fourteenth, then I went to my father in Touraine, he was dying but hadn't died yet, all was calm.

16

I hadn't been to see him in at least a year. The house is a
wreck. Everything is falling down. There's dust spiderwebs
his too-white face. The electrical outlets don't work.
Everything is broken. In the bathroom there is a hole
under the bathtub, missing tiles, and the plug is jammed,
I wedge it out with the section cup of a toy arrow to empty
my bath every morning. He's seventy-eight years old. You
might say it's a miracle. He watches series on the iPad in
the afternoon but in the morning he listens to music on
his telephone, old stuff on YouTube. I ordered him some
Bluetooth speakers, I am sure that will be better. We talk
about Rutebeuf, Villon, and Rimbaud when we talk, for a
few seconds, and then we go back to not talking. Yesterday
he wasn't feeling well. Even with the oxygen. He always
says he's cold. I say Yes, it's cold, even when it isn't. He says
he's dying, I don't dispute it. He says That's how it is, I say
nothing. What else can I do apart from not responding

and buying him frozen Bounty bars and Snickers at the supermarket. At night I hear him struggling to breathe, I wonder how long a dying body can hold out. I found a copy of the *Chants de Maldoror*, Éditions Corti, 1969, two prefaces, one by Soupault, talking about bourgeois houses and clutter, and one by Gracq, which says "a princely and native disgust of reason and order is the privilege of an eternally anarchic childhood." What can you do. You can cry or you can laugh, Bacon said to Hockney the day of his huge exhibition at the Grand Palais, the day after the death of his lover George Dyer, and he laughed.

17

I didn't witness my mother's death, I read about it. In a book my father wrote. He goes to meet her in a café, she feels dizzy, she has him call a taxi, she lays down in the back, she rears up, she says she can't see anything anymore, he takes her to the ER, he says My wife is dying, he's right, she dies. He never told me the story. I never asked him about it. I read it once.

I didn't see her dead, I didn't want to. They gave me the chance, before they unplugged her. They also asked what I thought about unplugging her before they did it. My uncle the doctor, in my grandfather's study. I said Yes of course. I went back to the living room. My sister wasn't there. My sister wouldn't be informed until the next day. My father was in the living room. He didn't say anything, he helped himself to some whiskey. Crystal bottle. The slab of black marble atop the Second Empire sideboard.

The portrait of Arago, white ascot against a black background. My grandmother smoking, who says when my father pours himself another one It's pointless to drink, my father shrugs his shoulders, my grandmother does the same, has the same look on her face, lights a cigarette with the butt of the previous one, her legs crossed, as she always does. My sister comes home from school. No one tells her anything. We slept in the same bedroom at my grandparents'. They told her the next day after school. She howled. When I opened the door to my grandparents', she threw herself on me and howled. I saw what it was to be a broken person, a broken child, I can no longer tolerate children screaming.

The burial was a few days later. In Touraine. Clothes had to be bought for me. A skirt. A blazer. When we arrived at the church, with all those people looking at us, my sister began to howl again, so they took her home. I stayed with my father and all the people looking at us. It was repulsive. Everything was repulsive. My father crying. The priest spouting nonsense. Talking about children dying of hunger in Africa. The stupid coffin resting several yards from us, where everyone could see it. The church. The people. The things the people said, It's too young to die, forty-six, It's too young to lose your mother, sixteen (me) and eight (my sister). The people who looked at us to see if we were crying or not. Their pity. The idiot vicar. Shut up do you hear me, shut up.

18

When she comes to Paris, my mother's mother stays at the Lutetia or the Meurice. We go to see her as if attending an audience with a visiting dignitary. She comes once or twice a year. She leaves the Landes for dog shows or on business. She and my mother speak English on the phone. So as not to be overheard by the maids or whoever might be listening in. They speak English in families like theirs, even if they never leave their châteaus. My mother sings me nursery rhymes, One two buckle my shoe three four shut the door, we go to the Tea Caddy near Notre-Dame, we have Christmas crackers that we buy at WH Smith that come with tissue-paper crowns that I wear. My grand-mother breeds dogs. Since my grandfather died, it's become her passion. There have always been dogs and kennels in that family. Or horses. She calculates the breeding. Never shows any tenderness. Short gray hair, a Pall Mall hanging from her lips, turtlenecks, polo shirts, tweed skirts, chin high. No part of her is submissive or apologetic. My mother takes me to see her when she comes to Paris. Hello Granny. We don't pronounce it Gran*nee* but Gran*nay*. She calls everyone *tu*, calls children *mon chéri*, boys and girls alike. A woman of few words. Chin high. She always gives me a 500-franc bill, no envelope, no shame. The men in the family are at the Jockey Club. She lives in the Landes. A shepherd's house on her brother's land near his own château. My grandmother's house. I remember three bedrooms. A bathroom with red water because of all the rust in the pipes. A large room. Always servants. I went once. My aunt lived there too. The one who drank eau de cologne. My grandmother was born in London, her father was an attaché at the embassy in the early years of the century, the twentieth. She grew up between the *hôtel particulier* on the avenue Matignon and the château near Castres whose name she bore. At her own funeral, at the foot of the burned château where I was baptized, only two out of four daughters remained. Alcohol pills drugs, every time. Not a cent remained.

19

We don't say Eat, we don't say Enjoy your meal, we don't say Hello without adding the person's name, if I were a boy I would know exactly when it is and is not appropriate to kiss someone's hand, and when to send flowers, and we don't talk about the food we're eating, and we don't go on and on about nothing, we're always fine, and we are very kind to servants, we don't call the waiter sir, we leave tips, we're never overdressed, we're never ashamed. All these manners, these good manners that I know by heart, I hate them. I hate them because they are ingrained in me, deeper than my blood, they are more than a language, they are a body, they are my body that allows me to recognize other bodies like mine and those which are not, which annoy me with their poor-people's anxieties, their poor-people's complexes, their blunders, their vulgar way of being obsessed with class, with their poor-people's taste and their belief in good taste, with their poor-people's ideas about rich people, I know as rich people do how little rich people care about money, that it is only poor people who talk about money, who talk about food, when I say *poor people* it's because it's easier that way, because if you know you know and the rest will never understand, I detest these class-conscious manners which make me classify people according to their manners, I hate these good manners, which are like the grit under my nails, they can be read in the way I move, the way I speak, the social class that makes me sick is my own, embedded more deeply within me than a tick feeding on my skin. I want nothing to do with it, but I belong to no other, I know it very well. I hate these good manners because they prove that they've won, people who believe in classes, that this family, with its disdain for people who aren't like them has always made me sick, has won, that there's no cure for it, that you can detest other people but loving them is harder, that what I would like is people who don't come from any background but you only find that in people who have left everything behind, maybe, but because at a certain point they had everything and they know that it means nothing. I hate these good manners which prove that I can fight as much as I want but I am firmly bound in these filthy bourgeois trappings for life, for life, for life.

20

No money, no house, no inheritance. It's part of my philosophy of not leaving anything behind. Not even my name. I thought about it as I was filling out the paperwork after he was born. I'm not a cow breeder, I'm not branding anybody. Let him have his father's name, ordinary and transparent. A name that doesn't concern me. I have spared him my own. None of that. It's better. In a society which is finally modern there will be no more names. No more names and no more inheritance. But modernity is endlessly late in arriving.

I no longer see my son very often. These are the kinds of things that happen when you change your life. Maybe it will get better and maybe it won't. Maybe it's somewhat serious and maybe it isn't at all. What does that change. What can you do. I'm used to it now. It's a condition like any other. Part of the rules of my game.

I have a political agenda. I am in favor of the elimination of inheritance, the requirement that ancestors sustain their descendants, I am for the elimination of parental authority, I am for the abolition of marriage, I am in favor of children getting some distance from their parents at as young an age as possible, I am for the abolition of filiation, and for the abolition of the family name, I am against guardianship, minority, I am against patrimony, I am against having a domicile, a nationality, I am in favor of eliminating the *état civil* of your name, date and place of birth, parentage, and marital status, I am for eliminating the family, I am in favor of eliminating childhood as well, if we can.

I think that what has happened doesn't matter. Things that happen in childhood have nothing to do with childhood. The slightly bitter taste like the taste of blood in the mouth has nothing to do with the things that happen. It's just the taste of childhood. That's how I see things. I never think about childhood. That is, I never think about the taste of blood in the mouth that came to me long before anything happened, that came with childhood itself. Children detest childhood, that's all. We have to remember that when we become adults, when it's left us, when we've finally freed ourselves, how lucky we are. To no longer taste blood.

21

I studied law. I did it to understand. Not to be a lawyer. Being a lawyer came later, when you had to choose a side. People in my family make the law; I prefer to plead against it. People in my family are on the side of the winners; I prefer the losers. But before anything else, I did it to understand. That's how I function. Sometimes it takes me a while. Take my body for instance, it took me forty years to understand what to do with it. That I should stop obstructing it. Say yes or no and be done. I want or I don't want, for everything, a dinner, a lover, a career. Without having to justify or explain myself. I studied law to be able to understand the world, to know the law. To understand how law explains the world. The way law rules the world. Really. Concretely. Inside and out. Unlike philosophy, which is only in your head. But in real life. In people's real lives. In their heads because the law is in their heads, and of course in their bodies and their lives. Because the law is concrete. Because it's everywhere. It's so completely every-where that we wind up thinking that it's what we think. When it's in fact the law. When it's in fact order. The outside order which seeps into people's minds, their bodies, their houses, their lovers, their sexualities. It's the law that shapes people. Everyone should study it. It makes you stronger. Poor people especially, to be able to speak on an equal level with other people. But poor people don't study law. They don't do anything they ought to. They don't study anything, or they study only what will help them get a job, nothing intelligent that helps them refuse to get a job and be strong. To arm themselves with the weapons of the adversary. I have lots of ideas like that for poor people. It's not that I care about them. It's that they make me ashamed. It's frequently been a problem in my love life. Girls who go on believing that they're poor. To behave like poor people, believing in rich people, believing that it means something to be rich. I try to show them, they don't understand, it takes all their imagination, I end up leaving them or they leave me. You can understand a lot of things with the law. The minor is irresponsible, he can't make his own choices, he's like a madman, an idiot, senile, he's like women were thought to be for ages and in some small way he's like a slave, a foreigner, undocumented, he's like an animal, an object, he's powerless, indebted, subju-gated, constrained, a kind of prisoner from morning till night. As far back as I remember I hated childhood for that reason. Not because of my childhood, because of childhood itself. The childhood in childhood. I will never understand why so much importance is given to the only time in our lives when we can choose nothing for ourselves. Everything begins when it ends. If the world were well designed, upon turning eighteen we would forget everything, we would never see our parents again, we'd change our names. Papa-Maman is a slave's cry. Eighteen years inside. Eighteen years is what you get when you kill someone.

22

It's summer, I swim, I work, I live in other people's apartments, other people's homes, in the homes of people who have gone on vacation and left me the keys. I don't fuck anyone, I don't see anyone, I don't talk to anyone. If I grab a quick coffee with Jibé, there's no need to talk, we don't say very much. I don't have a girlfriend, I am very attached to the idea of not replacing the last one, it will happen eventually, it always does. I love solitude so much that I really have to keep an eye on myself, I could happily live always alone, I am always alone, even when I'm with someone. Sometimes it seems as if I could forget the woman I love, forget she exists, that the smallest distraction would be enough to make me forget about her like I might forget my keys in the door or my cash in an ATM. I pay attention, it doesn't happen but it could happen, there is a place for that within me. I do not 100 percent believe that love is some huge thing, that's what I think, more like 90 percent or 99 percent or 32 percent or 51 percent, it doesn't matter, but not 100 percent. People will tell you anything about love, they're lying when they say it's this enormous thing, immeasurably large from bottom to top, lengthwise widthwise and diagonally. It's not true. It's not difficult to say that love is also a small thing, a very small thing, and even that there is a place where love is totally absent, where there is nothing, where the person we love doesn't appear at all, we don't care the slightest bit about them, we don't even know her name, she doesn't exist. It's not difficult to say because it's true, because everyone knows it, because everyone feels it. What's wrong with what's true, what is their problem with the truth, I always find myself wondering.

On a bike, I'm riding a bike, Paris is empty, it's the summer, I listen to Bach, two preludes and a toccata, always the same ones, I go for a swim at Georges Hermant, behind the Buttes-Chaumont. I go at lunch, when no one is there, I've even ended up getting friendly with the manager, I stay for coffees in his office. I hardly read anything. There are things that disgust me and things that don't. I only do things that don't disgust me. Swimming, riding, listening to Bach, reading Manchette or Deleuze, avoiding people, owning one pair of jeans and two T-shirts, living in other people's apartments, doing yoga on the Down Dog yoga app, €8.99 a month, peaceful warrior, eagle pose, drinking Coke, eating dates, buying blue

Malabars for twenty centimes each at the corner shop, shaving my head every eight days on setting number 2. There are things that disgust me. An infinite number of things. So many I could not list them. Even books, sometimes. To an unimaginable degree. To the point that books themselves could be said to epitomize all my disgust at once. To incarnate what is disgusting to me about everything. In the apartments I move through, I see books, the right books, I can't touch them, I arrange my gaze so that it does not land on any of them. If I were a terrorist, I would begin with the books, I would destroy them, I would tear them all up, I would burn them, all these well-organized books, these little walls of books, these little apartments of books, these little cities of books, the arrogance of books, the flabbiness of books, the bourgeoisness of books, the sluttishness of books, all this decoration, the fake plaster, the fear, the cowardice, the stupidity, the stupidity of books, the immense stupidity of books, of those who read them, of those who write them. It's so fundamentally grotesque, all this brouhaha around literature, it's grotesque because it's not true when you look at how the people who make it or read it live, you can see that something isn't right, that there is nothing true there, that it's always the same miserable lives, that it doesn't change anything. There are days when the disgust rises in my throat, disgust at books, disgust at love, disgust at everything. There comes a time when you have gone so far into disgust that you no longer care about anything at all. Other people. The pain of the world. Poor people. The people we love. Injustice and death which have always been there. What you find obscene is those who are still offended by it. That is what disgusts you, their indignation, their sorrow, their complaints, their tears.

The smell of chlorine, a Peugeot bike, a Bach toccata, an outdoor pool, Speedo logos on backs, crawl stroke. I left my room in the fourteenth without realizing it. I left it a few months ago. Then came Perpignan, the few weeks at my father's. I came back, I stayed at my place for a few days, then I got out of there, without really thinking about it, because I was offered other apartments, in other neighborhoods. At first I thought it was only for a few days, but I went from flat to flat, and the days turned into months, and I no longer crossed the Seine, I stopped going to the Left Bank. First I stayed with Antonia on avenue Trudaine, because she was in Corsica. Then at P.'s, in the same building. I don't know her very well, I met her at the café downstairs, we had a drink, she was also going on holiday for a week and offered me her place, I said yes. Then I went to stay at A.'s, three weeks by Goncourt Métro station, I watched her cat. Then at L.'s place in the eleventh, near Couronnes, a bachelor pad, my favorite kind of place. I didn't go back to the studio in the fourteenth, I thought about it and I realized it was over, that it ended on its own, that all that was left to do with the place was to give notice, move out my stuff, return the key. Soon it's September, people are coming back, I'm leaving, I don't know where, I'll find something, it's not important. I understand people who have got too used to being nowhere to accept walls. My father is in the hospital in Tours, he's dying, I should go and see him, I don't go.

23

I've lost count, I can't recall all the names of the hospitals he went to for treatment. Sainte-Anne, Saint-Mandé, Cochin, La Membrolle, regular hospitals or day hospitals, clinics, methadone centers, rehab centers, postrehab centers, in Paris, in Tours, near Paris, near Tours. How many different places over thirty years, coming in through the emergency room or the front door, thirty, fifty, one hundred? My father's data should be recorded somewhere on his Social Security account, unless they erase it all when you die. Places for junkies, places for crazy people, places for old people, places for whomever or whatever. Good places to take a break, to get some rest. We go to see him, my sister and I, each on our own, with no one else. I bring him crime novels, cigarettes, razors; we talk about books. There is always a coffee machine, the smell of the cafeteria. The guys we talk to in these places, if we talk in them, are always the kind who hang out by the coffee machine to smoke. We size each other up right away, we keep our distance, our indifference or our reserve, like in prison. These places are always vaguely ugly. Basic state insurance plan, my dad. What would he be doing with the fake luxury of expensive clinics. It wouldn't suit him, it wouldn't suit us either. As recently as five years ago the doctors were still trying to cure him. It was a little ridiculous but we didn't tell them. I imagine it was the only form of reasoning available to them; it was what they had been taught, they were doctors, they doctored. There was even a shrink who tried to get us to do family therapy. All three of us. I don't know what the point of it was supposed to be because we always got along well with our father. To help us understand him better maybe. As if we hadn't spent years living with him and his issues with drugs, alcohol, pills, we weren't shocked, we were used to it. It struck us as odd that the therapist would even try to understand why he drugged himself, what we thought about it, what it was like for us, his little family. It seemed absurd to me to try to find the cause of it. Causes are meaningless. So much less interesting than consequences. We went once, we felt like we were talking to a three-year-old, we spoke slowly, we were careful and measured in what we said, we didn't want to seem impolite by saying from the outset that we thought it was normal that he took drugs, that we thought it was normal to be the family we were, because all we could say from an objective standpoint, for many years, was that it worked. The therapist never called us back, or maybe we were supposed to call, or maybe my father cancelled the appointment.

That was two years ago. A year before he died. The Franco-Swiss clinic at Issy-les-Moulineaux. It sounds chic but it isn't. Before, hospitals were for drugs or alcohol. Now they're for real illnesses. Old people's illnesses, because he got old. Tongue cancer, for example. It doesn't change very much, it's the same atmosphere. The elevators are slow. One is reserved for staff. I get yelled at when I take it. I make trips back and forth to the coffee machine, to the vending machine, I buy him iced teas, peach flavored, or sometimes mint for a change. He is going to have an operation at the Salpêtrière in a few days but we don't know when. Meanwhile they run tests. They take him from one hospital to another. Last week he was in a clinic at Saint-Mandé. Now he's here. He sends me a text to let me know each time they move him. We don't know who's making these decisions or why, it's not very important, we go with it. My sister has moved to Touraine. I'm the one who comes to see him. It's always nicer to be him and me when he's in the hospital. He says I've been costing Social Security loads of money for years. He thinks it's crazy how much money is spent on old people, he thinks it's completely unreasonable from a public-spending perspective, he buzzes for more

Subutex, he says they're going to start giving him morphine, he says it's already that bad.

I go to see him every three or four days. He's part of my schedule, like the pool, like work. I like things that can become a discipline. I don't necessarily stay very long, just fifteen minutes when he's tired, sometimes we don't do much besides watch TV, we don't force ourselves, we're not those kinds of people. Even when it's just the two of us watching TV we're fine, we're calm, it's easy to fall back into old habits with him. I bring him books, Coke, yogurt drinks. Since he can't eat anything because of his tongue. We talk. Not for long. Not about anything. It's easy. We lead similar lives, he and I, we understand one another. Lives in which we do what we want, lives in which we don't care about much, by necessity. There was a report on Addis Ababa on TV at one point. He told me that Rimbaud's house was in Addis Ababa, that he had gone to see it, that there was nothing in it, a fake desk, a fake chair, copies of letters, a bad photograph, no doubt a scam. We talked about death, too, I asked if he was afraid, he said no.

Opium isn't heroin. Opium has nothing to do with heroin. On his hospital bed my father said repeatedly, as he always had, that opium had only advantages and no disadvantages, and that apart from the pleasure of it, it allowed him to discover many things, and helped rather than hindered him in his work, that he had never written so well, that his reporting had never been so strong, that he had never lived as rich and balanced a life as when he took opium, that everything was going well in the opium days, everything was a success. I think about it, I try to remember, maybe he's right, maybe he's wrong, what does it change.

Flo who shot up, Flo who became HIV positive when she turned to heroin. The last time I spoke to her on the phone was one New Year's Day. Not long after my mother died. I was living in a new apartment with my father and my sister, again on the rue Bonaparte, at a different number. My father took care of the move, he packed the boxes, sorted through our things, threw stuff out, put my mother's belongings somewhere, I don't know where, I never asked. I was alone in the apartment. I answered the phone. She was calling to wish us happy New Year. She was calling to say goodbye, too, she was making the rounds on the telephone, two birds one stone, she had been sick for a few months, she was going to die, she was dying. I told myself I had to ask how she was, that I had to be brave, I wasn't very brave at the time, I had to force myself. She told me. Her voice was calm. When we hung up I knew it was the last time I would speak to her. I really liked her ruined gray face, with its crevices, its hollows. The face of a junkie. I have always liked the faces of junkies. I don't really remember my mother's face at the end, I don't think she really had it. Or maybe hers was just different. There are lots of different junkie faces. My mother hadn't lost her teeth. If she had lived to be older than forty-six she might have but at forty-six they were hanging in there. Flo died a few weeks later. I really liked her.

In one of the three triptychs of Dyer's that he painted after his lover's death, Bacon paints death itself. A black shadow at Dyer's foot in the flat splatter of pink.

In *8½*, there is the sequence where Mastroianni/Guido talks to his dead father in a dream. He tells him that they didn't speak very much, that he has many questions to ask him, and the father replies that he doesn't know if he'll be able to answer them. I don't have a single question. I don't need any answers. My father told me he might not be able to speak if they took out a piece of his tongue but that they shouldn't take out a big piece. I asked if tongues grew back, he said no, and then we talked about something else.

Always the same dream, I'm burning my father, I'm starting a fire in a house in which he is not dead yet but not much alive either, he's almost dead and I burn him, I'm the one to kill him but all I'm doing is speeding up a process that has already begun, I strike the match, I light the blaze around his almost-dead body, sometimes my mother's body is also there, and I'm burning that too, but that doesn't really count because she's been dead a long time, and they both burn, anyway there's nothing I can do about their deaths, if the bodies burn what does it matter.

24

In July, avenue Trudaine. With R. He's thirteen but he looks about sixteen. His brothers aren't there. His mother whom I've known since university isn't there either. He chose to stay here rather than go to his father's. He's on his PlayStation. He goes to bed when he likes. No one bothers him, least of all me. We're alone, the two of us, in the apartment. I've been staying with them on and off like this for three years, for a few days or a few weeks. I started when I didn't have a place to live, and I've kept up the habit. There are times when I feel better at their place than at my own. You might say they're a kind of family. Even though I don't really know what that means. I know them all now, each son on his own, separate from their mother. Often when I'm staying there, before they've left for school or the office, I bring in croissants, *pains au chocolat*, they call me the breakfast friend, they ask if I got up early or if I haven't gone to bed yet, if I slept there, if I'm coming from the pool or about to leave. I'm part of their land-scape, they're part of mine, I have the key to their flat on my carabiner.

I go to bed early I wake up early. He's the opposite, he plays his video games sitting on the floor in front of the big TV in the living room. We cross paths in the morning when I'm waking up and he's going to bed. An hour when everyone is sleeping, when the light is grey. We talk very quietly because it's so early, doubtless because it's basically still nighttime. I tell him that I've always known about him, that I've always known about who he is, that I saw it when he was two years old, that he's the kind of person who doubts everything, for whom everything is difficult and no one knows why. I don't tell him it will pass, I don't tell him he has to have friends, that he should stop with the video games, that he should do his schoolwork, I tell him that it's because he is the way he is and I am that way too that he plays video games and that I write books, that PlayStation and book writing are the same thing, I tell him that people like us are the ones who build the world that other people live in, even if they don't know it, I tell him that we're in the cave and we see the shadows, we know that the shadows are real and that they tell the truth about reality, that without the shadows and without us to see them there would be no reality, I tell him that it's pos-sible we may be shadows ourselves, that sometimes it's painful and sometimes it isn't, I tell him that I have no recommendations, that I don't have any advice, that for me it took years, I tell him that it's thanks to us that the world exists. He tells me they'd think he was crazy if he said everything he thinks in his head, so he doesn't say anything, he just plays video games.

25

A Sunday in November, a year or two ago. I slept at M.'s, badly. I'd gone out and came back late, we had sex for a little bit but I was so tired I had to stop, she let me sleep, it must have been 2 a.m. I woke up around 7. She was sleeping. Girls sleep. They don't wake up. Or maybe they wake up and pretend to sleep, and let me leave.

I got out of bed by making the fewest possible movements, I tiptoed across the carpet, the parquet beneath squeaked a bit, I waited for some cars to go by on the boulevard so I could keep going, I gathered my things up into a pile by the door, I always do that, leave my things by the door, I took my bag my shoes my jacket, I opened the door, I closed it behind me. I put on my trousers in the hallway, my sweater, everything else, shoes, jacket, on the landing, there's no one else at this hour, I leave.

She worked as a call girl at university for a while. She worked in an S-M club on the weekends. She fucked for the first time when she was thirteen with an older guy, she wanted to know what sex was like. She had lovers and mistresses. Sometimes at the same time. She was sort of in a relationship with a guy, from what I understood, in an open relationship, I don't know if she saw him very often, I don't remember much about the situation, I mixed up her stories, I don't know how important it was, for her or for me. At the beginning I thought it might be interesting to go slowly like she did, not to careen toward an orgasm, I thought we'd figure it out because she'd always been so interested in sex.

At the beginning I came two or three times but barely, the kind of orgasm which hurts because it's missing one second, one more stroke for it to really explode. She didn't really come either. It was weird. Maybe it was too late to change, it had become our way, we weren't going to try any harder, there wasn't enough desire between us. Or love. Every day it got worse. But we still spent some nice time together. Like this, these weekends I spent at her place, in her room, she had a kind of sweetness, it was winter, I was coming out of a bad relationship, it did me good to be with her.

I left in the morning then I came back in the afternoon. That evening she suggested we watch a Chris Marker film. I was on her bed while we watched the film, I was wondering when I was going to be able to slip away, what I was going to eat for dinner. I was barely watching the film, there are certain kinds of films that I can't stand, the kind of culture that makes me think America saved us, that liberalism has some cultural value, I thought about that and about my dinner, and all of a sudden on her MacBook I saw my mother, in the middle of this black-and-white film, in the middle of this boring film, there is my mother with two of her sisters on the screen, my mother moving and talking, my mother who died thirty years ago, whom I've never seen move or speak since her death, my mother's face is moving, even though it's not the one I knew, not exactly, because she's nineteen years old in the film, even though it's not exactly the voice I knew, even though her sisters sound stupid and she doesn't say much. I said That's my mother. I said it again. That's my mother. I must have said it four or five times. I didn't say anything else. How does it make you feel, the girl asked me. I didn't know how it made me feel. It's stupefying, I said. I am stupefied. It's all I could say. I am stupefied. It is stupefying. To see her. Or to remember that all that existed. She. She and I. She for me. She was everything. And then nothing. I tried to find something other than stupefaction, I couldn't. Not that day and not since. Nothing else is left.

26

I fill up the fridge I buy fruits, a jar of honey, I vacuum, I mop, I wipe things down, I wash the sheets, I dry them at the laundromat, I put them back on the mattress, I empty the dishwasher, I close the windows, I leave a note on a Post-it, I leave the key on the Post-it, I take my black Eastpak with the broken front pocket that holds my white T-shirts, my gray boxers, my toothbrush, my computer, my things for the pool, the rest of my belongings, the jeans the Converse and the T-shirt on my body, I slam the door, I take out the trash, I get on my bike, I head out, the Canal Saint-Martin, the Gare de l'Est, the rue de Maubeuge, back to the avenue Trudaine, empty this time, in ten days I don't know where I'll go, in October maybe I'll have an idea, for September we'll have to see. *Les gens sans aveu*, "unowned people," that's how the Code pénal referred to people who had no fixed domicile, or work, or family, it was an offense, punishable with imprisonment, article 271 of the Code *et seq.* But that's the old law, all that is over now.

When I leave, be it a room, an apartment, a neighborhood, a three-day habit, or even a girl, it tears me apart, always the same way. What can I do. That's just how it is. I wouldn't know how to live another way. It's enough not to think about it, to block out the electric impulses in my brain, to rub my eyes, to ride my bike, to swim, it will pass, it's enough just to do what you've decided to do. It's enough to remember that you can live a calm life or an adventurous one. That if the adventurous one were always great, no one would choose a calm life. It's enough to remember that you've made the choice.

27

This Christ has the face of a killer and he wears Nike Requins. I've run into him a lot, in prison and at court, in front of judges, in the dock. Never anywhere but among the poor, never anywhere but among the guilty. These ones, the ones that made me think of him, these guilty ones, know that there is good and evil, that that's even all there is, that they are divided by a hair's breadth, a hair or a second. They are closer to good than the others, those who are unaware of evil. I don't know where this certainty comes from, or maybe it's more of an intuition, call it faith. They don't say that it isn't their fault, they don't say anything, they ask neither pity nor pardon.

Nike Requins, that's what he was wearing the day he killed the old lady. J. has a gypsy name, whereas hers is a proper French one, with an old-fashioned first name. He's barely eighteen. Seventeen stab wounds with an IKEA knife, the same one everyone has, four for €2.99. They're in every apartment I've stayed in. Every time I check, and I think of the old woman in Blanc-Mesnil, of the photos of her face up on her linoleum, her dress pulled up to reveal her old-lady underpants and her large white belly, the wound gaping at her throat, the black stain and the sea of black blood all around her, everything I saw in the police photos, everything that could be seen or imagined a few months later when they did the reconstruction. It's no easy thing to cut someone's throat, especially with a small knife, even the medical examiner had trouble understanding, he wondered how he could have had the strength to go so far, right up to the trachea, cut all the way through, while leaning over her the way J. had said he had, he said it wasn't possible. For a murder, a suicide, or a breakup, it's not possible they said, although it is possible because it happened. I liked the old lady a lot, J. always said, and they didn't understand that either. He was the only one around who could help her out from time to time, take her to do her shopping, or to her physical therapist, he nicked a little bit of her shopping money but he liked her a lot. There was the being held in police custody at the main police headquarters, the visiting rooms at Fleury, the interrogations at Bobigny, the criminal court. A nasty trial where I achieved nothing. Nothing got through that week, not his Gypsy face, not the old lady's body, not my arguments. For a week I keep running up against that wall. The closed faces of the jury. He couldn't care less. When I turned to him, when we chatted during recesses, he made jokes, he seemed happy to be there, indifferent to the trial, happy to see his mother in the audience, to chat with me, it distracted him. The trial, the sentence, it seemed like he couldn't care less. After the verdict, I told him to appeal, he said no, that it was fine, I shook his hand, I said good-bye, he seemed happy, he wasn't angry with me, not with me, his lawyer, not with the jury that had found him guilty. I remembered his name and I typed it into my email. I hadn't kept my legal files because I don't keep anything. I threw it all out, just as I throw everything out, photographs, mail, same with all the messages on my phone after a breakup. But in my email I found fragments of the file, what the court clerk had sent me, an official statement of transport, another for the reconstruction, the interrogations, and then an MP4 file, a recording that Apple had saved despite the fact that I'd changed phones several times since then. It was at the drop-off point, in one of those jails in the basement of courthouses where they keep the defendants while they wait to appear before the judge, those jails guarded by gendarmes or policemen, depending, those jails where lawyers can go down to have a quick conversation with their clients in a visiting room thrown together in a corner. On the recording you can hear doors opening and closing, the police and prisoners as they come and go. We started off talking about his detention. How are things, you always ask first. He had been in solitary because of the weed, he smoked a lot, his mother had been caught bringing him some during their last family visit. He said he wasn't sleeping, that he couldn't sleep anymore, he said that every time he slept, he saw the old woman, he saw the blood, that it scared him awake, that he didn't dare go back to sleep, he said that he smoked so he wouldn't see the blood, to dull himself, to manage some sleep. He said that he kept reliving the events in his head, that he was trying to understand how he came to be there, killing the old lady, that he was retracing his steps, that he was going crazy, that it was pointless to be crazy, that that was just how it was, that all he could manage to want to do was to sleep. He didn't care about the trial, he didn't care about the sentence. Sometimes justice doesn't mean much, not for the victim or the one who is punished, justice is usually meaningless, except for those who exercise it, so to speak. I have often felt that what happened in a courtroom had nothing much to do with what was being judged, with facts and people, that it concerned justice, the judges, the State, those who were in attendance, not really those who had suffered or those who were judged, that they were at the periphery and not the center, that no one cared about them. I recorded it, you're not supposed to but I had done it anyway, without telling him, with my phone on the table. In prison, lawyers are supposed to leave their phones at the entrance, but not at the courthouse, not at the drop-off point. At the sound of his voice I remembered his face, very brown, and his missing front teeth. I remembered the file, which told about Blanc-Mesnil, his girlfriend, their baby, his father's one-bedroom apartment where they lived, the afternoons at the stadium with the stroller, his friends, the weed, the weed that everyone smoked, the nights playing video games, his sick father, his brothers, the plans to move to Nantes, his childhood, the years when he had been in care, as all the kids in their family had been, at one time or another, not that anyone knew why, and what came next, because of course it did, the dropping out of high school, the criminal record, light though, only one item listed, receipt of a stolen scooter, age sixteen, nothing really, next to nothing, the stupid kind of life that everyone lives in these kinds of places, neither better nor worse. That's what surprised the judge, she was a good judge, it can happen, it doesn't change much but it can happen, she said that the violence of the murder was out of proportion to the kind of life lived previously, not great but not the worst, like the others. She's right, a guy like him usually does some time, of course, but for petty crimes. When she interrogates him, he replies, he speaks, he tells stories, he doesn't explain anything, there's nothing to explain. Why him and not the others, the judge wonders, and I wonder why not the others, I wonder why violence like that happens so rarely, with their awful pointless lives. He didn't apologize at any time, not in front of the judge or the members of the jury, he said nothing, he waited for it to be over, I think he thought it was completely normal to be punished, I think he would have thought it dishonest to apologize, that you can't apologize for something like that. There have been others like him. I've defended dozens of guys like that with stories like his. I listened to the recording, I reread some things in the file, and the next day I went to Foot Locker in Barbès, I bought some Nike TNs. Jesus sneakers, I thought, then I left for Touraine to see my father who was dying.

28

At the Relais H at the Tours train station I buy three Nordic crime novels by Jo Nesbø, and two Cokes, one for him, one for me. Building A, pulmonology. Second floor, room 260. From the threshold, before I've knocked or gone in, I can see his hands, he's holding his iPhone, he's watching a series. I knock, I go in. Hello hello. He's a little thinner, not much. Not dead yet. Now it's his lungs. They're trying a new treatment, we don't talk about it. I don't ask any questions. He's getting out in ten days. He says he can't be alone at the house anymore. That social assistance is trying to find him a place in a care facility. I tell him to go home to Montlouis, that I will be there, that I was planning to come in September anyway. I don't tell him that I'm doing this for him, I say I'm doing it because it's convenient for me, and in a way it's true. He says OK, he says I should get going, he says he's tired. The whole thing lasts seven minutes. I get going, I walk toward the station, it's hot, I get another Coke, I buy a sandwich, these things always make me hungry. An hour later I'm in Paris, Gare Montparnasse, I think of my flat which isn't too far away, I tell myself I should stop by, clean out my stuff, in ten days I have to return the keys. To Barbès, Marlboro Marlboro the Arab vendors say, I always wonder who buys them, I walk two blocks to avenue Trudaine. Antonia's apartment. She isn't there, neither are her sons. The big rooms, the Milanese design, the mouldings. I shave my head, as I do every week, bare torso, pale and thin, I look at my body my face my tattoos, I would never be able to keep going without all that. Being beautiful has nothing to do with women, it's not about other people, I am beautiful for the same reason they do push-ups in prison, for the sake of honor.

29

She is lying down in the water, her stomach to the sand, arched up on her elbows, she's wearing a bathing suit, she's looking at the sea she's not looking at him. We see that he's looking at her, and she's letting herself be looked at, we see that their love story has something to do with beauty. For him. For her as well. The photographs are in black and white. He took the photos, always. Photos of her. Not vacation photos, no photos of Greece. No photo of them together, no photo of himself. The writing, too, on the back of the photos, belongs to my father, Mykonos 62, in pencil. In the photos he doesn't appear. Not in these or in the ones from later, the ones in the albums in a cupboard in Touraine.

They met in Athens at the home of the ambassador. My father had gone with his father the prime minister on official business. My mother was on vacation with her sister, the ambassador's name was Humbert, like in Nabokov, and he was her uncle. They were twenty years old. For two weeks or maybe a month there was nothing but the sea, the sun, and themselves. When they said goodbye at the end of the holiday, they didn't exchange telephone numbers, they knew they would run into each other again, Paris is very small, etc. At parties, for weeks my father heard things like She just left, She was supposed to stop by, You missed her by five minutes. Then they found one another. They were together ever after. They argued, they separated, they got back together, they never left each other.

In a copy of Rimbaud's *Illuminations*, in the countryside, each phrase of "Royalty" is underlined.

> One fine morning, in the land of a very gentle people, a splendid man and woman shouted in the public square: "My friends, I want her to be queen!" "I want to be queen!" She laughed and trembled. They spoke to their friends of revelation, of ordeals completed. They swooned against each other. Indeed they reigned a full morning, when the crimson hangings were raised against the houses, and all afternoon, when they marched toward the gardens of palms.

From the very start they were lovers like that.

Once, in the early years, they tried to break up. Really tried. Not like all the other times before or after when they tried but their hearts weren't in it. Like her later. He left and went as far away as he could, he preempted the call to duty, he went to Madagascar to serve his mandatory military service doing volunteer work. But she came to see him in Fréjus where he was doing his training, he snuck out to meet her. After that it was pointless to resist. Pointless to take the boat, pointless to put the Indian Ocean between them.

In Madagascar, he loved a girl. A very pretty girl. He still has her photograph, in a closet under his jeans, my sister found it and showed it to me. There was this girl but it didn't change anything. She also had a lover, I believe. But that didn't change anything either. They wrote to each other every day for a year and a half. That was also where he tried opium for the first time. In an opium den run by an old Chinese man. The girl had brought him there, he had asked her about it, she got some information, found the address and the contact they needed to get in. It's something he'd wanted to do for a long time. Which had made him take a whiff of ether when he was a teenager, one summer in Brittany, while his brothers played tennis went fishing were sailing, while they asked themselves how they were going to be their father's sons. Meanwhile he was waiting for childhood to be over. He only wanted that, to get out.

One day after their umpteenth breakup, one that may have lasted longer than the others, they got back in touch, they decided to get married, to have a family, a child. I was born.

30

In September my job is my father's death. He left the hospital, they let him out to die, I came the night before. It's organized like a Mass. It happens slowly. It's quiet. Unsentimental. Dying has a precise schedule. There are objects, people, things to do at certain times of day, acts to accomplish. There are very few phrases but there are words. Oxygen machine, medical bed, nurses, nurse's aide, medication. Skenan, vials of Oramorph, protein drinks, chocolate, coffee, vanilla or hazelnut, urinal, commode, light sedation, deep sedation. He doesn't say anything, I don't either. My sister comes by. Sometimes alone. Sometimes with her children her baby her husband her dog. She cries. She wants to tell him things. She asks if he's said anything solemn. She wants to tell him solemn things. She says she'll come back tomorrow. Her husband says Call me, don't hesitate to call. I don't say anything. My head hurts. I have grown unaccustomed to families, I have grown unaccustomed to dogs, I have grown unaccustomed to phrases. My asthma is acting up, I use my inhaler, they leave. It's quiet again. I am alone with him again. I go into his room. Everything OK? He nods. Or he makes a joke. Don't ask any stupid questions. Funny, OK. I charge his phone. At the beginning he's still watching series. At night sometimes he coughs. Sometimes he calls me. Generally he doesn't. Generally it's quiet. I buy a three-door Peugeot, diesel, with 197,000 kilometers on it, an old 206 with a cigarette lighter and an ashtray. Swimming at the Centre aquatique du Lac on the way to Tours Nord. Run in the vineyards. When we ask how long, the doctors say they can't answer. On Instagram a girl I don't know sends me messages at night or very early in the morning. I write back to her. The weather is nice. I sun-bathed yesterday. It's cold at night. It's September. I messaged my son to let him know. I didn't get a response. My sister talks about me as if I hadn't changed at all. Maybe she hasn't noticed. Maybe it reassures her. My sister her husband her children. My way of living seems to open up a gulf, between me and other people. My old client, old seventeen stab wounds, sends me a message from prison on a prison phone. Hello I'm fine and prison is going OK and you how are you? What's up with you? I hope your new life is good and that you're enjoying life, if you want to talk to me that would make me happy, speak soon.

My father tells me to make all the decisions, my father tells me to call the doctor, he makes a gesture with his hand, I understand but I ask him to spell it out for me anyway. So they can give me my fix, he says. I call them. We can do that, he and I. We can talk about death, he and I. With very few sentences. No tears. No comments. What can other people do for us, a journalist asked Francis Bacon one day. Stay beautiful, he answered.

He asks me to cut his hair. I've never cut his hair before. Normally we don't touch, my father and I. He sits on the side of his bed, I place a towel around his neck, so thin, his white hair so beautiful, the hollow of his thin neck, we don't say anything, what the fuck are we doing, all of a sudden it's unbearable, I cut a few locks, he tells me to stop, I say OK, we don't say anything. I take away the towel and the few locks, I look at the white hair in the towel, the word *relics* comes to mind, I throw the locks in the trash in the kitchen.

In the afternoon, my sister. She comes by for lunch. She's trying not to cry. She shows him the baby. When she comes I go swimming. Peugeot. Tours Nord. Centre aquatique du Lac. Crawl stroke, two kilometers. She doesn't know that my father and I are talking about death, how we're organizing it, how quiet it is.

Morning evening night. He opens his eyes, I'm sitting on the edge of his bed, he says It's strange. Strange how? He says it's indescribable, that it doesn't really hurt. He repeats Indescribable, he says it like something coming from the inside of him, he says it like this new sensation really interests him. At night he calls me, I go down the hallway, I stand at the foot of his bed, I answer him with a few words. Him, me, death, what has to be done.

The dying man tells me You make all the decisions. The dying man every morning tells me Call the doctors. The last mornings the dying man tells me Talk to the doctors so they can do what they have to do. To increase the doses.

The pumps. The steel IV stand. Two hooks. Two plastic bags, transparent, with liquid inside. Morphine and midazolam. Tubes leading from the bags to my father's stomach. Subcutaneous. There are devices like joysticks to release a push of morphine called a bolus. *Bolus*, new word. A bolus is permitted every three hours. A sedative bolus and a morphine bolus. I touch the screen for the pumps, I control them, I put my hands on the joysticks, beep goes the morphine, beep goes the sedative. My father is completely white, he looks like Proust on his deathbed but without the beard. Or maybe he looks nothing like Proust but just like a dead man on his deathbed. He already has his dead face but still has his alive face. But he's getting more and more white, more and more dead. I give him as many boluses as I can, I send him all the boluses, all the poison possible, even when he's sleeping, even when he doesn't ask for it. At night I wake up every three hours for it. Beep go the pumps that send the chemicals into the body of my father. Death is a video game, PlayStation or Atari. I go up to him at night and during the day to see if he's still alive. Every three hours I touch the screen of the pumps, I pick up the joysticks, I send him another dose, I watch my father get more and more white, more and more dead, I go back to sleep.

I know that he'll die at night, and not during the day when my sister is there. I know I'm the one who's going to find him dead during the night. He won't do it while she's there. I didn't see my mother dead. His death will be for me. At night, the girl I don't know yet writes to me. I write back to her. She says she has two sons. She says the death of the father is the job of the firstborn. He uncovers himself, it seems they do that when they're going to die, something about the hands on the sheet, I remember Céleste Albaret says something similar in *Monsieur Proust*.

My bedroom in the study at the end of the hallway, the cold tiles, the dust, the open books, never closed, never put away, books from the spring when I was here with him, books that belong to this house, his and mine accumulating for a long time now, an old Henry Miller, a stained Michaux, some crime novels from the '80s, bought no doubt at Le Drugstore or La Hune, insomniac nights, his or mine.

Four a.m., I wake up, I missed the 3 a.m. bolus, I was sleeping. I get up, I walk down the hallway, I don't hear him breathing, I go into his room, I turn on the flashlight on my iPhone, I point it at his chest. His chest isn't moving, I watch it for a long time, verifying that he's not breathing, watching his thin white chest that isn't moving, looking at his face, dead, banishing the image of his chest rising and falling that superimposes itself on my retina, I put the back of my hand to the back of his hand, it's cold, I slip my fingers around his cold wrist, there's no pulse, I watch him again, I wait again, I leave his room, I follow the clear plastic cord of the oxygen machine, all the way to the living room, I lean over the gray block of the ventilator, I press zero.

31

I would have written the same book with any other parents. With any other childhood. With any other name. I would still have the same thing to say. That you have to escape. From wherever, however. Escape. Get further and further away. Geographically or without moving. Be more and more alone. Go toward solitude. Your own or someone else's. It is possible that what lies ahead will destroy the old structures, the family, the couple, love, work, everything we've learned. Possibly we will need to prepare ourselves to be much stronger, to survive it all. Possibly we will need to learn to live differently, to no longer have faith because any threat could topple it all. Possibly we will need to learn to live like animals or warriors, for long periods of exile. Possibly the world to come will need heroes. I would like to put myself forth, literature can be a useful model, that's why I write in the first person.

The hero's life is full of corpses. Not everyone is up to it. My sister isn't, that's why she got married and has three kids and a dog. Most people aren't. I am. That's how it is. Say Adventure. Say Literature. Say Love and death. It all happened at the same time, love and death, my father and Camille, at the same time.

While he is dying, while I am calling the doctors, while they are administering morphine and sedatives, while they are upping the doses, while I am getting up at night, finding him dead, while the undertaker and the funeral are happening, we are writing back and forth, early in the morning, at night, during the day as well. We have never met, we don't know each other, we write back and forth. She calls me St. Aug. She writes c u later. She says that she doesn't know how to leave girls, that she puts her tongue in their mouths to stop them talking. Being with girls is still a little new for her though not completely. She has lots of stuff lots of friends lots of clothes. But often at six in the morning she writes to me. Before her workout, her meetings, her job, her taxis. While I am with the dying man, I reply to her. She is what I don't yet know.

C. went quiet for twenty-four hours after his death. At the end of twenty-four hours she asks how the pain is. I don't feel any pain, I feel the opposite of pain. She says Death is OK. Without disdain or pity. She says Are you coming back? I say Wednesday maybe.

After the funeral there is Paris, there is Camille.

She says that she died thirteen years ago. She says it in her messages, before we've met, or maybe on our first date, before we've kissed. We meet on a café terrace. She's wearing an old raincoat, some military-style shorts. She says C'est weird, I say Of course not, she says we're going to drink and then smoke. She describes her death, the Xanax the vodka the nurse the people. We talk, it started to rain, it rains and rains, my Church's are little pools of water, we're soaked. Who cares, she says. How many glasses? Red wine. Usually I don't drink, tonight I'm drinking. I said I'm going to kiss you, we kissed a lot, we kept talking, and kissing more and more, her thighs under my hands, I said Invite me over? Or maybe she was the one who said Are you coming over? Her son wasn't there. We slept together on her big couch, her thin muscled body was light and hot, I said Do you want me to leave? she said Absolutely not, we slept, her body against mine, she took my hand, that was what most surprised me, the way she slept against me, months later it continued to fascinate me. As well as the list of her friends, lovers, husbands, mistresses also a bit. She's not the kind of girl who says thank you, or I love you, she's the kind of girl who is uncomfortable with saying serious things and she only says serious things but lightly. I say that but really, I don't know, what do I even know, it's only the beginning.

Camille is every morning and every evening. Every night she says Yes of course, to whatever I suggest. Or she's the one who suggests it. She never says that she has a dinner or she's meant to see friends. Ten days like that, in Paris. I sleep at the flat on avenue Trudaine but mostly at her place. The word *love*, of course, is never spoken.

I leave for Arles. An apartment for three months. A writing residency. Naturally I said yes. Once again fill up the tank, hit the road, the trucks, the rain, the rest stop, rest stop coffee, tire pressure, black on my fingers, smell of gas, of coffee, cigarettes, sounds of the motor, the windshield wipers, or the radio. It's still dark, then gray, then blue. Names fly past, highways. More road and then Arles. I park at the lot at the center. My bag on my shoulder. Julie B. gives me the keys, I push open a door, I pass a porch, a courtyard, a stone stairway, a large studio in an old tower, a fireplace, the roofs, the sky, the light. October and then November and then December.

Again her nighttime messages, when she wakes up, when she goes back to bed, then again early in the morning. When she goes out as well, when she has a dinner or a social event. She talks, she writes to me, but she says One day I'll tell you why I don't say anything. When I ask her the question later at Arles one of the first times she comes, while she's sitting near the fireplace and I'm on the floor, we've been drinking, she looks at me, she says I'm not going to answer. Maybe later still she'll give me the answer in a message when I'm on the train, when I've come to see her one night in Paris. Maybe she will discuss it with me again. There are some questions you can't ask.

I get a tattoo on my ass that says St. Aug. I swim, by the Lidl, at Guy-Berthier, or at Saint-Martin-de-Crau, near the highway. When the pools are closed, I run, I cross the Rhône and head toward Trinquetaille, toward Fourques. The sky above Arles, the blue the wind the light. It makes me think of New York, of winter in New York. Raise your right hand and swear, they told me at the American consulate on the avenue Gabriel, when we had to renew my son's passport. I saw him at my father's funeral. My son who is a little bit American, like C.'s sons are a little English a little German. Sometimes, early in the morning, I take the car, I drive through the Camargue right up to the sea, I don't run into anyone apart from a few fishermen, the water is cold but not yet freezing, on the way home, at the Bar des Sports in Salin-de-Giraud, I order a double espresso at the counter, I leave, I drive some more, I listen to the radio or a CD, Bach, the only CD I found in Montlouis. Coffee at Virgile every morning otherwise at the Bazar otherwise at the Café des Gitans with the alcoholics, at first they gave me weird looks but now it's OK. I swim I run I see no one I work and then I often go to pick up Camille at the train station.

Avignon TGV, drop-off at the curb, blue Peugeot. She watches me while I drive. Bag of wood at the Total station. Fireplace, wine, night. She says she calls me Prince Constance. She says that she tells her exes that I am the ideal man. Every night, in the tower, she sits by the fireplace, she puts on some music, she is very particular about that, and then she talks. Every time she comes, she talks. Sex all the time. Wine. Music. The list of her lovers. The list of her lives. Sometimes I go to Paris. I decide when I wake up, around 6 a.m. I get in the Peugeot, train, hop on a Cityscoot at the Gare de Lyon, by half past noon I'm having coffee with her on a bench. She says Stay, and I stay for two days, she says You'll stay with me of course. And she comes on the weekends. She comes more and more often, she stays longer and longer, she always says yes, she says Take me, she says Do what you want with me. She comes at Christmas and we spend two weeks together, more and more we're living together, I return to Paris, the word *love*, of course, is never spoken.

32

I could have had a father, a mother, brothers, sisters, an astrological sign, a life line on my palm, an Ayurvedic type, a blood type, a religion, opinions, I could have had a favorite color, I could have had a lucky charm, a talisman, icons, idols, I could have had wounds, longings, complaints, regrets, I could have said I'm from a generation, a country, a city, an era, a class, I could have laid claim to a gender or a sexuality, I could have sought a way to define myself, I could have believed in identity, or gone in search of my own, I could have been a victim or a culprit, I could have said J'accuse or Mea culpa, I could have looked for my roots, a reason, a why, I could have believed in genealogy, in sociology, in DNA, gone looking into the rabbis, the noblemen, the Basques, the ministers, or the junkies, I could have believed in all of that, I could have had deep pockets, I could have gone to see a shrink two times a week, I could have asked him to help me to want all the things I don't want, I could have asked him to cure me. I live without property without family without childhood.

33

I live on the boulevard de Clichy near the Monoprix where the serial killer of Eastern Paris Guy Georges was arrested, not far from the elevated train at Barbès above where Guyotat parked his camper van to write and fuck. I live between Love Story and Toys Palace. At the twenty-four-hour supermarket there are poppers next to the candy, I buy Coke and ice cream bars, every day I say See you tomorrow, every day they reply Inshallah. Studios, plural, I'm getting more bourgeoise, six flights up it's good for your ass, with a view, from here the Left Bank is beautiful. The Tour Montparnasse blinks blue at night, the city below looks like LA. Around 5 a.m. it's often pink, unless it's gray, or bluish white. Camille lives ten minutes away, five if I cycle. I got back my brown Peugeot bike. Parked the blue Peugeot car in a lot. In the car I listen to CDs. CDs that she gives me. We tried them the afternoon of the 31st on the drive back from Marseille, and when I left Arles at five in the morning and drove all night back to Paris I listened to them all. Go and get him, she said over Christmas in Arles, talking about my son. I have seen my son again since I've been back. I went to pick him up one day as he came out of school. Since then we've been seeing each other. At her funeral she wants "Bela Lugosi's Dead." Sometimes we sleep at my place sometimes hers, sometimes we don't sleep together but that's rare. At her place there are piles of books, heaps of objects, a huge painting. A nineteenth-century family portrait, coat of arms upper right-hand side, the same as on her signet ring. A young woman, some children, a little Black boy. She says The way they would have added a little dog, to make it pretty. There is a cross-shaped scar on the face of the great-aunt, she stabbed the painting of the family one evening, drove a knife into the great-aunt, she says That's what's funny, she says *funny* a lot, to mean lots of different things. In Arles the first or the second time she came, at a tattoo parlor in Beaucaire, in a garage, she got a tattoo on the inside of her left hand, like a crucifixion, like a nail plunged through her hand. She leaves the light on in the hallway at night. Often her son is there, the younger of the two, we have dinner all three of us, everyone's careful, we're all a little intimidated.

I can't do it, I can't go toward sadness like she does, to each their own settings, their own operations to maintain order against chaos, that's why I don't drink, that's why I swim. Individual with extraordinary ability, that's what the American government said on her O-1 visa. She thumbtacked my picture onto the door, the big one on the cover of *Les inrocks*, next to Lemmy and 2Pac, her sons, some of her exes, Only the heavy hitters, she says. Sometimes she comes when I'm sleeping, she has the key, she doesn't warn me, she doesn't turn the light on, just the flashlight on her iPhone, she undresses, she gets into bed with me. Now I too sometimes have my son to stay. When can I read your books do you think, he asked me, I don't know, what do I know. When we don't have our sons we're together, we're together all the time in fact, now she's the one who mostly comes over here, to my studios. I'll be leaving the boulevard de Clichy soon. I have to go to New York for a few months. I'll relinquish my studios. Trade Pigalle for Chinatown. When I come back we'll see. Camille says she'll come to New York. It's like taking a train, the way I live. Swim, write, sex, these are techniques to make some things exist and disappear the rest. Camille is also a train. Something that I won't stop doing. I don't tell her that, it would sound like a promise.

34

Les Vedettes, place Pigalle, one morning. Rather die than what? he asks me, we're strangers, he's thirty-two years old, a third of which he spent in prison. Réau, Fleury, Nanterre, he lists the names, another six months of parole, meetings at the probation office, the SPIP, Service pénitentiaire d'insertion et de prévention, they speak in acronyms, we're talking about disgust, Rather die than be disgusted maybe, he says my book isn't long enough to be about disgust, maybe he's read some of what I've written on the pages I'm going over alongside my double espresso, what disgusts him is a third of his life, what disgusts him is the white bulletproof vest under the black shirt he unbuttons to show me, level 3 he wants me to know, what disgusts him is no longer being able to love, the insomnia, having developed a sun allergy, he says What a stupid allergy for an Arab, he says that things have changed, that everything has changed, he was born in Paris, he says it wasn't like this when he was a kid, he says he doesn't know if it's him or if it's Paris, he says that what he would like is to get away, in six months, when his parole is over, he talks about England, Australia, Italy, to leave so he no longer runs into the police, the judges, so he no longer runs into the guys from his neighborhood, he says he has to go, that the coffee's on him, he asks me What can be done? I don't know, what do I know, leave, start over.

ABOUT THE AUTHOR

Constance Debré left her career as a lawyer to become a writer. She is also the author of *Playboy* (winner of the Prix de La Coupole, 2018) and *Love Me Tender* (winner of the Prix Les Inrockuptibles, 2020), both published in English by Semiotext(e).